Other Books by Rebecca Weber:

The Painter's Butterfly

Loophole

Rebecca Weber

Illustrations by:

Sarah Ann Doughty

ISBN: 9781963832099 (paperback) / 9781963832211 (ebook)
LCCN: 2024945981
Copyright © 2025 by Rebecca Weber
Cover illustration © 2025 by Sarah Ann Doughty
Interior illustrations © 2025 by Sarah Ann Doughty
Cover Quote: Isabel Allende

Printed in the United States of America.

Kinkajou Press
9 Mockingbird Hill Rd
Tijeras, New Mexico 87059
info@kinkajoupress.com
www.kinkajoupress.com

Content Notice:
This book covers several topics related to mental health and well-being including anxiety, physical abuse, death of a loved one, and betrayal. We understand that such descriptions may trigger your own fears and anxiety, however we also hope that the story within these pages can provide you with the tools needed to help you face your traumas either alone or with the guidance of a trusted friend, family member, or therapist.

Dedicated to my amazing mother, who taught me how to use my voice. I love you, Mom. Thank you for always raising us with tender, loving care.

And to her best friend, Tammy Sagona, who understood the power of books and embodied unconditional love.

Also, to Jailyn. I never met you, but I won't ever forget you.

Loophole: an ambiguity or inadequacy in the law or a set of rules.
- *Oxford's English Dictionary*

MAMA WAS ALWAYS TAKING: "medicine," phone numbers, half-fulfilled hopes—anything and everything. As if she was trying to fill up some kind of hole inside her, but it only got bigger and bigger.

All she ever gave me was my name, and I'd call even that a half-gift. The alphabet has twenty-six letters with endless combinations. And she chose Maybelline, the weirdest of all names. I could depend on Mama to be impulsive.

According to family lore, her labor lasted for three whole days. I finally showed my face on April 1st, like fate knew how foolish Mama could be. The prank was actually on me. When the doctors asked my name, she had no energy left, except to apply a new coat of ruby red lipstick. Thank goodness it wasn't Lancôme.

"Call her Maybe. Short for Maybelline. She's my first."

And, as it turns out, her last. The pain was so great, Mama had an operation to stop her from having more babies. Probably for the best.

Since moving to Salem, Illinois to live with my aunt and uncle, I haven't made any real friends. I've got my cousins, Lyla and Lucy, but they overlook me like an old wind-up toy. Especially since the silence.

But I'm getting ahead of myself.

My name's Maybelline Reed.

Reed fits me more than Maybe, with a small tweak. I'm *reading* my way through the library's collection of kids' books... halfway through the C authors. Should be on to D by the end of summer.

In September, I start middle school. I am not looking forward to it. Too many people, especially boys. Fingers crossed I can convince Aunt Julie and Uncle Mars to keep home-schooling me. This mess is the new therapist's fault. She thinks the "exposure" would be "beneficial." Two big words with lots of implications.

That's what nobody understands: I'm not hiding. Well, not really. Mostly, I'm trapped, because the last thing Mama took from me (before she left) was my voice.

I haven't spoken aloud since the beginning of the silence. Not in five whole years—one thousand, nine hundred, and fifteen days to be exact. But really, who's counting?

Only me.

Chapter 2

Keep-the-anxiety-away Rule #1: Neatness matters.

THE OFFICIAL DIAGNOSIS—ANXIETY and obsessive-compulsive disorder. Thirty-four letters with a million consequences, all windy and jumbled inside my overactive mind. They tangle with the intensity of an EF5 tornado, while I stand in the eye, watching my life's debris fly past. I flick my eyes over to a wooden clock on the wall, praying the therapy session is nearly over. My lungs deflate as I realize an eternity to me has been nothing but seven minutes.

The steady whirr of a white noise machine and subtle hint of lavender permeating the therapist's office are meant to clear my head, but nobody understands my internal struggle. Even with two feet solidly on the floor, the storm never stops. Not for a second. My brain operates independent of my will, circling round in an endless loop of worries, evidenced by the dark shadows under my eyes and my nubby gnawed fingernails. Like that tornado plucked me from the ground, to whirl until the rest of the world turned upside down. I *click, click, click* on my pen, to release some of the mounting tension. The blank paper in my lap intimidates me like a column of looming clouds.

Turbulence ahead.

I scribble on the edge of my notebook to fill the void, glancing at the back of Miss Mendoza's head out of the corner of my eye. Even my scribbles have purpose: beautiful curlicues and patterns, weaving together like a well-built bird's nest.

"How's that list coming along, Maybelline?" Miss Mendoza's lilting voice breaks the clock's endless ticking as she spins around in her swivel chair, her shiny black hair fanning out around her shoulders like a dancer's skirt. I hold up my spiral notebook, empty but for the swirly doodle in the upper corner of the page. Tilting forward, wavy blonde hair cascades in front of my face as a protective shield. *Click, click, click* goes my pen. I wait.

Miss Mendoza chuckles. She clasps her hands neatly together, like folded wings, and sidles next to me for a better look. The smell of her perfume, tart as fresh-made lemonade, tickles my nose. I hold back a sneeze and squirm on the overly fluffy couch.

"Lists can be hard when you don't know where to start. How about I help out?" Her slender fingers come into view under the fringe of my hair. I hand her the notebook, and shift further back on the couch, muscles going slack as a loose rubber band. For now.

"You prefer cursive, yes?" she asks, situating her skirt.

I nod my head once, and she starts to write—*scritch scritch scritch*—against the paper. I swear the clock has stopped ticking completely.

A robin perches on a branch outside the window; a wiggling worm clasped in its beak. Three chicks pop up out of a twiggy nest, and the mama bends to feed them. Mamas are supposed to take care of their young. A lump settles in my throat, and I rip my gaze away to go back to clicking my pen.

"Small steps are the best steps on this journey. I'm proud of you for meeting with me today." Miss Mendoza leans closer, and I do my best not to flinch. She hands the notebook back to me. Her notes are as beautiful as her jade green eyes and ebony hair. The writing is elegant, but elongated on a slant. I skate my brown eyes across the letters as if on an icy winter pond. My finger longs to trace them.

Things I'd like to change:

Things I'd like to stay the same:

Miss Mendoza glides across the room, skirt rustling against her ankles, and taps a few keys on her silver laptop. Peaceful harp notes echo from speakers situated on the nearby bookshelves. Then she reclines in an overstuffed chair kitty-corner to the couch and smiles.

"You don't have to fill in your list now. I'd much rather you think about what details would fit into each section." Miss Mendoza leans a little closer. "With starting middle school, I also want to revisit the possibility of medication. Have you thought any more about trying medicine to help cope with your triggers?"

My tongue sticks to the top of my mouth and I shake my head vehemently NO. Mama took too much medicine and nothing good came of it. I won't be like Mama.

Miss Mendoza pats my shoulder. "We don't need to try medicine until you're ready. I understand why you feel so strongly about it. For the rest of our time, let's practice breathing together. You can lie on the couch, and we'll take a deep breath each time we hear a bell in the music."

Reluctantly, I lie down and close my eyes. My body sinks into the couch and I stiffen like it might swallow me.

"Breathe in, hold for three seconds, and then breathe out," she instructs, and a bell chimes.

I take a shallow breath in, hold it, and then release.

We continue the routine, and I admit some of the stress melts away. The worry tornado gets a little less windy but keeps twirling in the background, spinning memories around until they smack me, demanding my attention.

"Breathe in."

Mama's manicured hand in mine, walking home from the supermarket. I grip the pen more tightly. My knuckles turn white.

"Breathe out."

The tiny apartment where I used to live, fuzzy around the edges like a faded photograph.

"Breathe in."

The antiseptic hospital smell stinging my nose. Mama sleeping in a white bed, me staying quiet so she can rest.

"Breathe out."

Fiddling with my suitcase on Aunt and Uncle's front porch as Mama argues with Aunt Julie around the corner of the garage, far enough away they think I'm out of range, but close enough I can still hear their anger. A robin circles over the house, making eye contact with me as I wait, wait, wait.

I jolt awake when a hand lightly grips my shoulder. A blurry Miss Mendoza bends over me and I blink back to life, clinging to the citrus perfume.

"You did a great job, Maybelline. We'll practice breathing the next time you visit too. Deep breaths are an effective tool when you feel overwhelmed." She smiles so big her eyes crinkle at the edges, and against my better judgment, I believe her. That lump within my throat has disappeared.

"If inspiration strikes, work on your list and bring it back next week. You can wait in the front room while I chat with your aunt." Miss Mendoza opens the door, and I scurry out of her office. A burst of cool air blasts goosebumps down my arms. Aunt Julie stands rigid by the front door but softens like melted butter when she sees me. She pats my back and scans my face, as if searching for buried treasure. I give her a crooked smile. She's trying her best.

Aunt Julie presses a paper check against the wall and adds her signature to the bottom. Her cursive is always pretty, but usually rushed. The letters meld together like a piece of gum stuck to a hot sidewalk. She doesn't let us chew gum, being an orthodontist. But her writing is ooey-gooey and sweet when she slows down and pays attention.

As the grown-ups talk, I study my notebook. Writing means communicating without noise. I add my thoughts to Miss Mendoza's list. My cursive is tiny and unobtrusive, but precise as I can make it.

Things I'd like to change:

   Going to middle school

   Mama

Things I'd like to stay the same:

Chapter 3

Keep-the-anxiety-away Rule #2: Avoid boys at ALL costs.

UNCLE MARS DOESN'T COUNT. If given the choice between public middle school and homeschool with my uncle, I'd choose homeschool in a heartbeat. *'If it ain't broke, don't fix it. If it is broke, call Tech Dude.'* Uncle Mars' motto. And I'm broke as can be.

I've tried to convince Aunt and Uncle all summer that I'm better off staying home for school. Less anxiety equals less distraction and better grades. But they won't budge on the issue. Middle school is apparently non-negotiable. Miss Mendoza may be nice, but my current situation is all her fault. Frustration burns in the pit of my stomach, and I bite my fingernails while I read the same printed sentence from my textbook over and over again. More of those endless loops. Ugh.

I shove my nose further in my book, while Uncle Mars zips through the kitchen, balancing dinner preparation with his most recent job: a wonky smart watch on the fritz. The king of multitasking, he stirs a pot of chili while examining the broken watch under his magnifying spectacles, a.k.a. ginormous glasses. The hot chili pops and splatters across his shirtfront, but he doesn't even notice.

Nobody tinkers better than Uncle Mars.

He's been helping me with homeschool since first grade, when public school got too overwhelming. Of course, the silence didn't help. Hard to participate in class when you don't talk. And even harder to make friends. Kids need the whole story to understand, and I'm not willing to share. Loneliness creeps cold through my veins like ice. Perhaps I'm better on my own. Uncle Mars works from home, so we established a routine where he'd work on his tech while I worked on my school. It took me a long time to get comfortable sitting at the same table, but we've fallen into a steady rhythm. I'm not sure why Miss Mendoza doesn't see the benefits of home-schooling. I've learned way more with Uncle Mars than I could learn in a classroom.

"Maybe, can you toss me the salt?" He reaches out a waiting palm. Uncle Mars' auburn hair sticks up at odd angles like he's been electrocuted. Can a busted watch electrocute you? Probably not.

Hiding behind my book, I snatch the salt from the table and throw underhand, aiming at the stove. The salt flies in the wrong direction, but Uncle Mars scoops it out of the air like a major league chef.

"And the crowd goes wild! Aaaaahhhhhhhhh!" He bows, his chunky glasses nearly dropping to the floor, before sprinkling the chili with extra seasoning.

My smile curls at the edges like one of Lucy's hair ribbons.

Snapping my book shut, I recline on the bench and my stomach grumbles. Uncle Mars stores the watch in his pocket and pulls a silver spoon from the nearest drawer, dunking it in the chili before offering the bite to me.

"A taste test, please, my lady."

A timid giggle escapes my lips. I can't help myself when it comes to Uncle Mars. He's not like other boys. It's tough not to love his goofy smile and endless string of dad jokes.

The chili explodes in my mouth, a perfect blend of garlic and pepper and chili powder and tomatoes. Licking my lips to catch every drop, I give him two thumbs up. Uncle Mars slaps his forehead and twirls around like he might faint.

"High praise!" he insists, before shouting toward the doorway. "Dinner's ready, fam!" He wipes his hands on his apron, snags a potholder, and places the giant pot of chili on the table. I bounce to my feet to collect bowls and silverware, then set the table in a mad dash to please my stomach.

Lyla enters first. Uncle Mars offers an arm to escort her to the table, but she rolls her eyes and flips back her edgy brown hair.

"Dad, you're so weird," Lyla mumbles as she nudges past him.

"But that's why you love me so much." Uncle Mars wiggles his eyebrows with a teasing smile. Lyla sits with a sigh next to me and buries her head in her phone. I stiffen when she scoots onto the seat. We're only a year apart, but everything about Lyla screams teenager. Dark clothes, brooding stare, and lack of enthusiasm for basically everything. She used to be fun, when we were younger. Now, she's mastered the art of ignoring everything. She sighs again, somehow more despairingly.

A pitter-patter of footsteps crescendos in the upstairs hall and speeds down the stairs. Not long after, my little cousin Lucy careens into the kitchen, wispy blonde hair flying in every direction. Uncle Mars latches onto her and twirls her around, ricocheting through the kitchen with matching boundless energy. The apple doesn't tumble far from the tree? Something like that. When he sets her back down, Lucy trembles with excitement.

"School starts next week!" she squeals. "Kindergarten, here I come!"

Lucy marches to the table like a soldier and salutes, before doubling over with laughter. Uncle Mars in little girl form. She sits across from me and immediately makes eye contact.

"School starts with S, Maybe. S says sssssssss." Lucy slithers her arm while she speaks. I try my hardest not to frown.

"Give it a try! You can do it! I believe in you!" Lucy reaches across the table and squeezes my hand. Her fingers are sticky. I grind my teeth together in a fake smile. Frustration bubbles beneath the surface of my skin, hotter than the scorching pot of chili.

"She doesn't want to, Luce. Maybe knows how to talk." Lyla doesn't even look up from her phone. "Stop being annoying."

Lucy's expression crumbles immediately. I give her hand another squeeze.

"I'm being a good helper. Helpers have lots of friends." Lucy shimmies her hips.

"Not if they're annoying," Lyla mutters under her breath. Uncle Mars fluffs Lucy's hair. "You're my amazing little punkin." Lucy beams full force in Lyla's direction.

"Amazing's a strong word," Lyla scoffs. "Have you heard her snore? The noise travels all the way through the wall to my room!"

"You don't have to be perfect to be amazing!" Lucy exclaims, waving her tiny pointer finger like the maestro of an orchestra.

"And all you girls are amazing. Don't you forget it." Uncle Mars winks, his open eye twinkling.

I blush and squirm in my seat, forcing myself to breathe. Too much attention, too little air. Thankfully, Aunt Julie interrupts. She pokes her head in the kitchen, cell pressed to her ear and palm against the phone's mouthpiece. "Go ahead and start without me. I'm waiting to talk to the principal."

My stomach drops as my personal twister gets stronger, and all of a sudden, I'm not hungry. There's not enough air getting into my lungs and my breath comes out in shallow gasps. Warning, middle school approaching! Gulp.

"Ten-four, honey!" Uncle Mars hangs up his apron and scoops the chili into everyone's bowls. "Bon appetit!"

Lucy shovels a heaping bite into her mouth.

"Meghan says that kindergarten is the very best grade." A bean spills from her mouth onto the table.

"Luce!" Uncle Mars tucks her napkin into her shirt like a bib. "Chew first, punkin."

"Yeah, not everyone wants to see your mushed up food," Lyla interjects. She spins her spoon around in the chili but hasn't eaten anything yet.

I close my eyes and try to breathe as anxious thoughts flutter to the surface like windswept leaves. Crammed in a building with a bunch of strangers, everyone staring at me when I can't answer questions, probably having to sit next to a boy in class. School is the last thing I want to focus on, but now the worry is so big that it squashes out anything else. Thanks, Luce. I grip the wooden table to stabilize myself as the wind whistles through my brain. When I open my eyes, Uncle Mars is looking right at me. I shove a spoonful of chili in my mouth, but now the food is heavy and tasteless. Swallowing takes extra effort. The silence spreads to everybody else as they notice my growing tension.

Aunt Julie returns to the kitchen. She blinks at the conversation-less table before breaking the silence.

"Lyla, no phones at the table."

Ms. Attitude huffs and slips her phone out of sight. Aunt Julie slides into the seat next to Uncle Mars, then places her napkin delicately into her lap before taking a first tentative bite. Her eyelids flutter closed, and she smiles.

"Mars, you've outdone yourself!" She rubs her stomach and chews slowly to savor the mouthful.

I try another spoonful and it tastes a little better. My heartbeat slows as the attention shifts away from me. As my body gradually relaxes, the gusts in my mind stop spinning. Uncle Mars may be the funny bone in the family, but Aunt Julie's the brains. She knows how to reach everybody, myself included, through some type of grown-up magic I don't understand.

"Might be my best batch ever!" Uncle Mars clasps his hands like he's holding an invisible trophy. "I'd like to thank the Academy."

"Mom, Mom, Mom! Guess what! In kindergarten, I get to ride the bus! Meghan says a hundred kids can go on the bus at the same time!" Lucy talks so fast that sometimes I can't keep up—and I'm the best listener I know. Context clues are necessary for understanding younger cousins.

"Sweetheart, chew your food so you don't choke." Aunt Julie chuckles and swings her concerned gaze to us. "Lyla, aren't you hungry?"

"Geez, Mom. I've got a little stomach ache. No big deal." Lyla flicks her hair out of her eyes and takes a tiny bite, grimacing. "Besides, I'm thinking about going vegetarian."

Lucy chimes in, "What's vegerarion?"

"A vegetable enthusiast!" Uncle Mars declares, while at the same time Aunt Julie says, "Someone who doesn't eat meat."

Lucy goes cross-eyed trying to absorb this information. Aunt Julie diplomatically changes the subject.

"First day of school is next week, so we'll have to pick up school supplies over the weekend. Your lists came in the mail."

Lucy vibrates even faster. A dark cloud engulfs me at the mention of school; my breathing goes shallow again.

"Ooooooooooooo! Do I need crayons and markers and paints? Can I get a yellow backpack? Yellow reminds me of sunshine!" I don't even have to look, I can literally *feel* Lyla rolling her eyes.

"Let's see what they've got at the store." Aunt Julie replies. "Lyla, you and Maybe should shop together, as a team. I want you to help her prepare for the first day of school. You remember from last year how overwhelming the transition to 6th grade was. Lots to learn. I spoke to your principal, and he's going to have you accompany Maybe for a few days during the first week."

Lyla's mouth falls open, speechless. Guess that makes two of us. I suck my turtle head back into the shell and try to quiet my racing heart.

A few blinks later, Lyla's back on track.

"But, Mom, I can't babysit Maybe the first week of school! I've got to learn my own schedule! Besides, what will my friends think if she's following me around everywhere? This is totally unfair." Lyla crosses her arms and glares daggers at Aunt Julie.

"Family comes first," Aunt Julie responds firmly, mouth set in a grim line. Lyla has the wherewithal not to press the point. Her furrowed brow quivers like a volcano about to explode, and she balls her hands into tight fists. Oh goody, she turns on me.

"You better not embarrass me at school." Lyla says, sticking a finger in my face to emphasize each and every word. "Don't act weird around my friends." Uncle Mars interjects, "Lyla, enough! That's no way to talk to your cousin. Go to your room until you cool off."

Aunt Julie shakes her head, disappointed, as Lyla whips out of her chair and stomps up the stairs. A loud slam shakes the ceiling, putting an exclamation mark on her rebellion.

"Can we find pencils with pictures on them?" Lucy says, without skipping a beat. "Meghan has pencils with unicorns."

Uncle Mars pats her on the head, but the attention is back on me. I burrow so deep inside myself that I don't bother to pretend to eat. My entire body tingles with fear of the unknown. The room swims and I put my face in my hands, willing the spinning to stop. My stomach twists and roils like I'm riding some sort of sailboat through a choppy sea. The waves are large and ominous, and I have to steer straight into the storm, life jacket-less and blinded with panic. What happens if the boat capsizes and I drown?

Middle school will sink me. I just know it.

Chapter 4

Keep-the-anxiety-away Rule #3: Speaking aloud is not allowed.

BY THE TIME SHOPPING Saturday rolls around, I need to get out of the house since it's physically impossible to jump out of my own skin. My mind cycles through the worst case first-day-of-school scenarios faster than the bicyclists of the Tour De France. I read about the famous race last year in a book from the library. Which gives me the inspiration I need. Grabbing my cloud-shaped whiteboard from where it hangs on my doorknob, I knock on Aunt Julie's bedroom door. Permission is paramount, there's no way around it. I won't be like Mama.

Aunt Julie sits on the bed while I carefully write my request on the white board. Though I practice my cursive constantly, the recent spike in anxiety makes me jittery. Cursive with a marker isn't easy either. My hand shakes with nervous energy, but I can't show her the question until my writing is 100% perfect.

Finally, I swing the white board around:

Can I go to the library before we shop?

Aunt Julie gives me a shiny smile. "Be back by lunch." Poof! I'm gone, tossing my white board onto my bed, then sprinting down the stairs and out the front door like my life depends on it. The library is my only safe space, no matter what stress my mind puts me through. The endless anxiety loops rule while I'm awake, but I can always depend on the quiet calm I find within the library's shelves to help soothe the panic. At least a little relief, and a little is way better than nothing.

Three whole blocks from our yard to the library entrance, and I jog almost the entire way. Kids of every age play at the park across the street, soaking up the summer sun in a last-ditch effort before the first day of... no. I won't think about it. My breath catches in my throat, and I trip on a crack in the sidewalk, nearly falling into the SALEM PUBLIC LIBRARY sign.

Though windswept and weather-worn, the blue-sided, antique building remains my everything, a lantern that shines bright through my dark reality. Truly a building only a reader could love. Grand and ornate, but long forgotten, it could pass for a haunted house if visitors squinted and tilted their heads. I've never known the library to get crowded... what with roof leaks, dust mites, and distinct old person smell, moth balls and cherry cough drops, lingering from floor to ceiling. I think most of Salem, Illinois buys their reading material online just to give the aging structure a wide berth. But the word that comes to mind for me personally would be haven. I wouldn't change a thing. *Light bulb*, and I draw a mental note (cursive, of course). I'll add the library to my list from Miss Mendoza as something I'd never change.

Taking the slouching steps two at a time, I land on the porch and it bellows a welcome with a mighty creak. Cuddles, the resident black cat librarian, lurks behind a potted plant, his two tufted ears betraying his covert sneaking. I purr at him before swinging open the hand carved six panel door. Purring doesn't count as talking. Besides, he won't tell anyone. Cuddles and I made a pact to always have each others backs.

The comforting aroma of old leather and years of disrepair settles on my shoulders, but instead of weighing me down, the familiarity makes me light as a balloon. A tin pail sits front-and-center in the tiled entryway, and one of the roof leaks *drip, drip, drips* into it, sending ripples of water in every direction. Below the surface of the water, daylight glints against a dozen shiny pennies, resting peacefully as if in slumber. Our allowance is five dollars a week, but I always get a dollar of that in pennies, to keep in a jar on my desk for easy access. You never know when you're gonna need a handful of wishes. I pluck another penny from the tiny stash in my pocket and toss it end-over-end into the bucket with a clink.

I wish Mama would respond to me.

I swallow the lump in my throat. To be honest, sometimes I hope I never see her again. But when I make a wish, it's always for Mama, which is my absolute biggest secret. I never wish the same wish twice. Everybody knows that would jinx it. Wishes are tricky and operate by their own rules. When you look hard enough, the entire world is built on rules. Rule-breaking means catastrophe. That's not gonna be me.

Leaning around the doorframe, I spy Mrs. Campbell in a thick maroon jersey dress nodding off at the front desk. Her dark gray hair rests in a bun, but splays to the side, with fluffy strands coming loose and tumbling down like hay from a scarecrow. She snores lightly into her hand, chest rising and falling in a peaceful rhythm. The towering shelves wait utterly still, not another living soul in sight.

For all my time in Salem, Mr. and Mrs. Campbell have run the library together. Mrs. Campbell's nice enough, but Mr. Campbell has always been a grade-A grump. He huffs and puffs if someone takes a book off the shelf and forgets to put it back in the right spot, and never lets anyone check out more than three books at a time. I try to click a pen that isn't there. Doesn't help that he's a boy. I haven't seen him in a few weeks, but previously I'd picked up the habit of avoiding him like the flu. Cuddles isn't the only one good at creeping around. I know the library like the back of my hand.

Tiptoeing past the front desk, I vanish behind the nearest bookcase, immersing myself in the beautiful blooming garden of stories. My home away from home, much to Mama's dismay.

I think I was four when I asked Mama to teach me to read. She wasted no time dashing that particular hope.

"Now, Maybe, why would you want to read? Get out in the real world, little lady, and have some actual adventures."

Mama didn't have time for books, and only occasionally had time for me. She was the one who had adventures in the real world. She'd put on her fancy dresses and strappy shoes, plant a kiss on my cheek, then leave me with Miss Tina next door. Miss Tina was the exact opposite of adventure. Her TV played soap operas 24/7, accompanied by frozen dinners heated a la microwave. Plus, she had a lot of old porcelain dolls hanging out on her apartment shelves. The way they stared at me made me shiver. Miss Tina helped me learn to read, but only because I wouldn't stop pestering her about it. Books whisked me away from that stuffy apartment; to places where Mamas love their kids more than anything else.

Apparently, my feet knew where they were going despite being lost in a daydream, because when I tune back into reality, I'm standing in front of three wooden cubicles housing boxy computer screens and crooked keyboards missing random keys. Blood pounds in my ears and I dig my nails into my palm, willing my rapid heartbeat to slow. First things first...let's get this over with. I boot up one of the computers and rest uneasy on the front of a chair, leaning forward like it might bite me. A bead of sweat trickles from my forehead onto my cheek, and I practice my breathing like Miss Mendoza taught me. Except someone must have taken all the air out of the library because my lungs aren't working right.

A few clicks and I've accessed my super-secret Gmail account, though I hesitate before typing my username and password. Deep breath. Best to get it over with. My story friends are waiting on the other side. But is Mama waiting too?

A quick tap of keys, a few clicks of the mouse, and I'm in. I sent Mama a message last weekend that read:

Dear Mama,
Summer's almost over and I'm nervous about middle school. Aunt Julie and Miss Mendoza think I should socialize, but I like being on my own. Deep down, I guess I want to try going to school again, but what if the kids don't like me? Do you remember middle school? Did you enjoy it?
I miss you, Mama, and hope you write back soon! I've

been practicing my cursive and can't wait to show you.
Love,
Maybe

But when I click into my inbox, there's no bold entry, no sign of activity, no glimmer of hope. Mama's last response remains dated three years ago. My heart crumples like a balled up looseleaf poem, and a headache pricks at my temples. *Where have you been? Do you even think about me? Can we still be a family? Are we still a family?*

Logging out of the account, my shoulders tense with disappointment, I drag myself over to the children's section of the library, past the bean bag chairs and toddler-sized oval table, to the stacks of middle grade reads. A quick listen ensures Mrs. Campbell snores softly up front, which means I've got as long as I want to explore these forthcoming adventures. I run my hand along the cracked spines, willing their warmth to counter the chill in my heart. Mama might not understand me, but books always do.

I've only got two titles left of the C's, and my stomach churns with the worry that public school means I won't have enough time to read. Tears blur the corner of my vision making it hard to see the titles. My knees almost buckle with the unfairness of it all.

I snag the next to last book on the C shelf, and hurry to the front desk, slamming the book onto the wooden counter much harder than I probably should have. A cloud of dust puffs into the air, and Mrs. Campbell bolts to attention, wiping a drip of saliva from her mouth with the back of a hand.

"May I have your card, please?" Her voice is groggy.

She blinks a few times, registers my face, and gives me a polite smile.

"Well, if it isn't my favorite reader! Maybelline, I didn't hear you come in. Quiet as a mouse! Sorry, I dozed off," she says, and reaches out a wrinkled crepe paper hand. "Do you have your library card?"

I yank my scuffed library card from my pocket and place it in her palm.

Mrs. Campbell adjusts her lopsided bun and scoots over to her computer monitor. She glances at me over the screen with a conspiratorial smile. "This'll be your fourth book, but we'll keep that our little secret." That's why she's my favorite.

She hands me the hardcover and I allow a shy smile. Mrs. Campbell pats my hand with grandmotherly affection, and tuts when she notices the time.

"Oh my! Nodding off turned into a full-blown nap! Tsk. Mr. Campbell would not approve." She giggles, but I frown. Mr. Campbell can be such a grouch.

"Speaking of Mr. Campbell, he's been downsizing his personal collection of books. Should've thought of this earlier, but it totally slipped my mind!" Mrs. Campbell reaches to a shelf behind her and tugs a black leather journal into view. She extends it to me, but I just blink, confused.

"Maybelline, you've read more books than anyone I know. Adults and children alike. Which tells me you've got a story hidden inside you. Think you can use this journal to get the tale down on paper? Better than an empty journal gathering dust on a shelf." Mrs. Campbell winks and slips the gift into my hand. The textured cover reminds me of the pretty pair of boots Aunt Julie got me for my tenth birthday. A seed of hope plants in my heart.

I cradle the journal to my chest, hoping Mrs. Campbell translates the enthusiastic thank you in my eyes. Her crinkly smile reassures me as I dash out the door. Hard to believe a piece of the library actually belongs to me. As I walk the three blocks home, the rest of the world melts away and the seed Mrs. Campbell planted takes root. A writer. I could write stories, like a real-life author. I'd never thought about the possibility before.

Taking a big sniff of the journal, I'm anchored by musty binding and a hint of cherry-flavored cough drops. For the first time since the announcement I'd be going back to public school, my mental loops slow down and the middle school gusts fade to the background, leaving me quiet to ponder my dreams. A tiny seedling sprouts toward the sky.

Chapter 5

UNCLE MARS LOVES THOSE old Western movies; the ones with bandits, sheriffs, and damsels in distress. Horses named Dusty, shoot-outs, and perilous chases between criminals and the law round out the equation for a perfect Western. For some reason, my brain latches onto this symbolism.

I'm the damsel, tied tight to the rusty track, and middle school is the gigantic train engine barreling down, growing faster every minute, steam hissing from its stack like a writhing mass of poisonous snakes. I open my mouth to scream, but nothing comes out. I've got no voice to ask for help. So instead, I'll wriggle and try to free myself. But each second that passes, the track trembles more, shaking like it can't handle the engine's speed. My teeth chatter as I rip at my bindings, fingers white with pressure, right before the moment of collision...

SCREECH. My alarm clock blares next to the bed, and I bolt upright, stiff as a board, sweat dripping down my back and breath coming in ragged gasps. Monday morning. The first day of school. A stone settles in my gut. Where's a heroic cowboy to set me free before I get squashed?

Can't depend on boys for anything.

Clenching and unclenching my fists, I summon my courage to get up and get dressed, slipping into a gray t-shirt and pair of jeans. I don't want to stand out. I take ten minutes to meticulously capture my hair in a perfect ponytail. *Appearance matters, Maybe,* Mama whispers at me from the mirror. Gotta look put together for the worst day of my life.

All right, maybe the second worst day. My mind spins like a washing machine, murky memories clogging my brain. My new tie-dye backpack hangs on the end of my bed, but now I wish I would've picked something less "look-at-me-I'm-the-new-kid." All my supplies are arranged neatly inside. But something important is missing... my safety net! I can't believe I almost forgot. I scoop the black leather journal from Mrs. Campbell off my desk and take a big whiff of the library scent, let it swirl around inside me and block out some of the worry. Perhaps it'll keep me from getting caught in my brain-twisting tornado. I stuff the journal into the confines of my bag. The library means peace, calm, and reliability. It will be waiting for me when this scary school day is over.

But what state will I be in?

Lungs tight as my ponytail, I shoulder my backpack (roughly a thousand pounds) and trudge down the stairs, reminding myself to breathe with each step. Clanging and chatter resounds from the kitchen. The smell of buttered toast and eggs makes me nauseous. Try as I might, I can't bring myself to smile when my aunt and uncle tell me good morning. Instead, my stomach churns and I have to sit down. Aunt Julie approaches, her eyebrows arched. She rubs my back. I must look worse than I thought.

Lucy and Lyla join the crew for my final meal, and I'm practically drowning. Everyone (even Lyla) won't stop talking about the upcoming first day of school, but only bits and pieces of conversation reach me through the growing mental storm. That's the hardest part of my loops...when they get bad, they can distort reality. How will I survive this?

Bus. Friends. Class. Shadow. Homework. Meghan. Science. Art. Assembly. Maybe.

Maybe.

MAYBE.

Blinking as the clouds lift, I notice the whole family staring at me, pale and wide-eyed. Aunt Julie was talking to me, concern etched across the wrinkles in her forehead. Lyla and Lucy won't meet my eyes. Uncle Mars jumps up and retrieves a banana from the counter.

"Here, kiddo. This should help settle your stomach." He cuts pieces of banana onto my plate like I'm a baby.

"Girls, I'll drive you to school as a special beginning of the year treat!" Aunt Julie announces, side-eyeing me while she sips her coffee.

Lyla shrugs, the movement barely discernible underneath her hooded black sweatshirt.

Lucy, however, puts on an infamous pout. "I want to ride on the bus! I've been waiting all summer!" Tears well up in the creases of her eyelids, threatening to spill.

I hold my breath in anticipation of a meltdown.

"Luce, we can walk to the bus stop, and the other girls will carpool!" Uncle Mars somehow shines a ray of sunshine through the dark cloud in the kitchen. How does he make everything feel brighter, and why can't I?

A couple bites of banana and a few minutes later, somehow I've wound up in Aunt Julie's SUV. Lyla's entire attention is aimed at her phone, so I lean back in my seat and marvel at the beautiful sunshine gleaming through the puffy white clouds, ironic on such a horrid day. The familiar neighborhood glistens in the daylight as Aunt Julie backs down the driveway and we're officially off. Destination: my biggest fear. A train whistle screeches in the back of my mind.

Somebody help.

Chapter 6

HARPER LEE MIDDLE SCHOOL.

The antithesis (that means opposite) of my precious, aged public library. Sleek, dark gray brick walls support the modern metal roof, all angles and straight lines and sterile atmosphere. Like a doctor's office… or a prison. Pulling into the parking lot, Aunt Julie goes extra slow to protect the hordes of students flocking toward the oversized glass entrance doors. I peep out the window, and soak in the chaos. My breathing goes shallow as if I'm watching some mind-bending catastrophe. The brain loops spin faster like a lasso, but I can't look away from the massive crowd. A train wreck in the making.

Aunt Julie parks her SUV in the drop-off line and shuts the engine off. Lyla's out of the car and onto the sidewalk before anyone speaks, combing the crowd for her friends. I concentrate on my breathing then unbuckle as Aunt Julie opens my door. Before I know it, she's leaning over and wrapping me in a tight hug. My body releases and I rest against her shoulder, trembling. A few tears drip from my eyes and onto her lacy blouse. She holds me even tighter. Aunt Julie smells of springtime—fresh air and roses in full bloom.

"You can do this." Her voice is feather-soft against my ear. "I promise everything will be okay."

When she pulls away, tears run in two thin lines down her cheeks. She sniffles a bit and so do I, before grabbing my backpack and hopping onto the unforgiving concrete. One foot in front of the other, I remind myself. One step at a time.

Somehow, I find Lyla in the crowd. She rolls her eyes and shoves a printed sheet of paper in my hand, motioning me forward, toward the entrance of the school. I speed read so I don't misstep: **Sixth Grade Schedule, Maybelline Reed**.

Students jostle each other to cross through the entranceway threshold into the towering front foyer of the building. I do my best to stay on my feet, timing each step with an extra breath to quell my rising fear as the river of people surges around me. My brain's gone so static I can't even process clear thoughts. This is really happening. Some would call it an honest-to-goodness actual adventure, but I have no idea how I'm gonna survive.

If only Mama could see me now.

Chapter 7

THE METAL CEILING SLANTS three stories above us, amplifying the noise in Harper Lee Middle School's entranceway like a terrible orchestra rallying to deafening volume. I cover my ears with both hands, the schedule brushing against my cheek, and hurry to catch up to Lyla. Except Lyla promptly stops walking, and I clumsily collide into her back.

She stumbles, but rights herself, then pivots to face me, daggers in her eyes.

I scrunch as small as I can while students breeze past us.

"Watch it," Lyla says, but surprisingly softens her voice when I flinch. Is that pity in her gaze? I don't know why, but an angry fire ignites in my belly. *Keep your pity to yourself.*

"Just chill. We've got to find your homeroom first. Super lame that I'm missing my classes, but middle school is nothing major." Lyla flaps her hand as if to ward off a pesky mosquito. A sizable lump lodges in my throat and refuses to move.

What do you know? All you care about is your dumb friends. But she's already turned away, peering down the hall after checking out my schedule. Without hesitation, she clutches my t-shirt and pulls me forward through the crowd, my heart hurdle-jumping like an Olympic athlete.

We patter across the speckled tile and around a few corners before Lyla veers toward an alcove with a door. The plastic nameplate reads "MS. BENNET" in all capital letters as if the plaque is yelling at me. There are a few kids milling about in the hallways, but most look like they're on a mission toward some final destination. I crane my neck to glance down the hall, trying to find a place to hide.

"Listen. We start in homeroom then find our lockers. After, we'll run through the normal schedule. Teachers never make you work on the first day. We just give each other introductions. So, sit quiet and let me do the talking." Lyla smiles when I register the joke. Now I'm the one glaring daggers.

"Whatever. Follow me." She shrugs, unfazed, and enters the classroom. I stay frozen, stiff as a statue outside the door.

Now's the moment to escape, to turn on my heel and sprint back through the school and into the parking lot. To run! My heartbeat drums in my ears as the hallway grows emptier, and somehow more foreboding. I could leave and come back at the end of the day, except Lyla would know I was missing. She wouldn't hesitate to tattle on me. I startle at movement in my peripheral vision, and my breathing goes shallow as I spin toward the figure.

A boy! (AAH!) His smooth skin glows under the artificial lighting, at odds with a black hoodie and dark jeans. Curly ebony hair spirals in every direction like a lion's mane. But most striking are his gray-blue eyes, eerily identical to the color of my t-shirt. He frowns and taps his scuffed-up sneaker to the floor. I cower, pressing close to the classroom door. "Just leave me alone," I want to shout, but all I can do is stare, open-mouthed and wide-eyed like I'm tied back on that rattling train track.

"Ummmm, you're blocking the door," he mumbles, hiking his clunky backpack further up his shoulder. Pivoting immediately, I force my feet up and down and straight into the classroom. I'd do anything to avoid confrontation with a boy. Rule #2 still stands.

Desks in neat rows face toward an enormous whiteboard peppered with colorful magnets and inspirational quotes. *Believe in you. Yes, you can! Hard work pays off.* The room's student population is divided into two camps: terrified-looking sixth graders sitting rigid at their desks, twitchy eyes forward while they fiddle with their fingers, and bold sixth graders reclining sideways off their seats and hollering at each other. I expect everyone to turn and stare at me, but kids are too busy talking. That boy edges past me to an empty seat, sending shivers up my spine. Lyla's claimed two desks at the back of the room. She hides her phone underneath her desk, fingers flying at the speed of light. I slink over next to her with shoulders hunched and perch on the edge of my seat, pulling out my black journal to anchor myself. My lungs crumple, so I definitely don't have enough air. It's all I can do to keep from wheezing.

A loud bell sounds over the speaker system and the teacher stands. She claps three times to get the students' attention, then strolls down the rows of desks.

"Good morning, sixth graders, and welcome to Harper Lee Middle School!" Her red ringlets sway against her face as she meanders about the room. She flashes a genuine smile at each student. Her teeth might be the straightest I've ever seen. Aunt Julie would approve. She stops next to Lyla and me, gazing over her crescent glasses in Lyla's direction. Lyla sighs and pockets her phone.

"My name is Ms. Bennet, and for many of you, we'll be studying language arts together this year. First thing in the morning, though, this is your official daily homeroom!"

A storm cloud swirls in my brain at the mention of multiple days glued to this chair. I hold my journal against my nose so the familiar library scent can lend me some much-needed calm. Still, my hands tremble while my mind runs laps.

Ms. Bennet plows onward, returning to the head of the class. "Sixth grade will be different from elementary school. You'll have lockers and switch between classes and be responsible for your own school materials and punctuality." She writes key words on the white board.

Organization, Accountability, Engagement.

Despite my panic, I'm pleased to see well-formed cursive lettering take shape. By her writing alone, Ms. Bennet may not be a total lost cause.

She claps her hands and grabs a squishy ball from her desk. "But, most importantly, here at Harper Lee Middle School, we know how to have fun! Before you find your lockers, let's play catch. When you catch the ball, tell everyone your name and then throw it to someone new." Ms. Bennet lobs the ball to the nearest boy, and he declares "Ethan" before tossing it across the room. Next up is "Susannah," "Grace," "Tony," "Carter". The game continues in quick succession, going so fast that I lose track of names after only a few throws. My interest piques when that boy from the doorway catches the squishy ball. He slouches in his seat, tossing the ball between his hands for a moment before answering in monotone, "Oliver."

Next thing I know, Ms. Bennet has the ball again and it sails in my direction. I reach out my hands instinctively to catch it. At the last second, Lyla stretches in front of me and nabs the ball. Shooting her a glare, I sit on my hands and retreat back into my shell. I didn't want to play the silly game anyway. So why does Lyla's interception bother me so much?

"I'm Lyla, but I'm actually an *eighth grader.*" The statement oozes from her lips, and she puffs out her chest before pointing at me. "This is my cousin, Maybelline. We call her Maybe. She's starting sixth grade and she's never gone to real school before."

False, but there's no way to correct her.

"Oh, and she doesn't talk," Lyla remarks flippantly before hurtling the ball back to Ms. Bennet.

My classmates lean closer for a better look, and my heart rate skyrockets. They ogle me like a goldfish in a bowl, and every nerve in my body screams for them to look away. I try to smile, but my teeth clench, stuck in a grimace.

"Lovely to meet you both!" Ms. Bennet checks her watch and claps again. All of my new classmates swivel around, and I'm free. My body deflates like a punctured balloon.

Lyla picks at a fingernail with a smug smile. At that moment, I want so badly to stomp on her phone to snuff out that smirk, or to tell the class she still sleeps with her favorite stuffed bear next to her pillow. Whatever would embarrass her the most, because I'm mortified. Reeling the thoughts in, I'm hit by an instant barrage of guilt. The temper flare-up reminds me of Mama. When Mama was nice, she was extra nice: she'd take me on trips to the beauty salon and we'd try on dresses at the mall. But when Mama was angry, get out of the way. She got mean. As in, nothing-for-supper and go-to-your-room levels of mean. Or yell-so-loud-the-furniture-shakes mean. Turns out anger can burn you from the inside out, because my tummy sizzles when I get mad. It's a wonder

Loophole

Mama never got burned.

"We've got about ten minutes left to locate lockers and prepare for first period! Please line up by the door and we'll head out! Go, team, go!" Ms. Bennet adds a little fist pump as students shuffle into the messiest line I've ever seen. I purposefully position myself way at the back, even though Lyla mingles with a few students in front of me. Forming a line so haphazardly triggers a distant memory, and my brain steers off the beaten path into my turbulent past.

****

Grade One in the earliest days of the silence. I'd moved in with Uncle Mars and Aunt Julie the previous May, when Mama had her argument in front of their garage. Being six equated to attending first grade, but there was just one problem: I refused to talk. Initially, my Aunt and Uncle ruled the lack of conversation "a phase," but my commitment to quiet during the summer proved them wrong. No bribes, discipline, or medical professionals could coax a single word from my lips. Fast forward to first grade in a new school with no friends. The teacher kept from calling on me for answers because she knew "the situation," and pretty soon the other kids caught on too. I was left to my own devices. To be honest, for a girl who missed her Mama, that powerful loneliness may have been the last straw.

Mid-November and our class had lined up higgledy-piggledy for gym. During lunch I'd guzzled my entire carton of milk and then got a long sip from the water fountain after recess, so my bladder was fuller than a turkey on Thanksgiving. I tugged at my teacher's hem and danced from foot to foot, a faint heat coloring my cheeks. The other kids chattered away, and she was too busy wrangling them to take much notice of me. Crossing my legs tight as a pretzel, I almost broke the rules to sprint to the bathroom without permission when everything... released. All it took was a second for the internal pressure to disappear. Warmth ran down my leg to the floor as complete dread filled my belly. I prayed no one would notice the puddle underneath my shoes.

When our line started to move, the kid behind me stepped with a splash into my puddle before stumbling backward, horrified, which turned into a domino effect that laid half the class flat on the floor like a set of bowling pins. The truth dawned on my teacher when she saw the mess I'd made, and she ushered me out of the room to the nurse's office, so they could call Aunt Julie to bring me fresh clothes. The hallway was long and echoey, and the other children's laughter chased after me. Hot tears cleansed my face, sniffles clogged my nose. I refused to go back to that classroom or attend public school ever again, deciding then and there I was better off on my own. Nothing my family did would change my loopy mind.

Chapter 8

911

SHINY NAVY BLUE LOCKERS stretch far into the distance like rows of jail cells. My locker, number 911 (really?), sticks and I use two hands to yank the door free. A solitary Cheerio litters one corner of the otherwise bare metal base. I brush it to the floor with my hand, then hang my backpack on the small silver hook without unpacking anything. I can access my books easily enough this way, and I withdraw my black leather journal and a ballpoint pen. No need to get overly comfortable. Thankfully, Lyla heads to her locker in the eighth grade wing, so she doesn't have the opportunity to bash my process.

The rest of my new classmates unpack actual decorations for their lockers. Family pictures, 3D magnets, fun mirrors, and ridiculous miniature shelves in every color of the rainbow. I brace my back against the cool metal door. How do these students instantly feel at home? Don't any of them have a nasty anxiety bug buzzing in their ear? My brain never slows down, always spinning like a rocket-fueled merry-go-round. Jealousy prickles my heart and I fiddle with my ballpoint pen cap, wishing I could click it.

When we finally march back to the classroom, we spend the end of homeroom designing name cards while Lyla practices her bored stare. We have to use markers, so the names stand out, but there isn't enough time to get mine perfect. The cursive ll's in Maybelline crowd one another like a two-headed snake. Ms. Bennet collects the name tags before I can rip mine into tiny pieces. Breaking Rule #1 (neatness matters) doesn't bode well for the rest of the school day. I cross my arms and wish my stomach would stop churning.

BRRRRNNNGGGG. The harsh bell reverberates again from the loudspeaker. I jolt and bang my knee hard against the underside of my desk. Rubbing my knee, I temporarily forget my sick stomach. Lyla, predictably, rolls her eyes as the students rush out the classroom door toward the next dot in their connect-the-dot schedule. Lyla drags me upright and pushes me to the door, before I limp into the churning chaos, head down.

My mind enters protection mode, floating above my body like a casual observer, following me from classroom to classroom as the day progresses: Science with frizzy Mrs. Quark where we review safety protocols for lab experiments. Math with stone-faced Mr. Kepler who plays with his Fitbit while we copy essential equations. And art with pot-bellied Mr. Remy. He has us paint a watercolor picture of our 'favorite place' that we'll hang on the classroom wall. My library's only half done when Mr. Remy collects the paintings to place on a drying rack. I resist the urge to ball it up and chuck the whole mess into the garbage can. My body sags against the metal stool, bogged down by anxiety's weight. My eyelids droop and I rest my chin on my palm, careful to keep my elbow away from any tabletop paint splotches. Perhaps resting my eyes would help...

A sharp jab in the ribs and I jump to attention. Lyla's elbow hovers close to my ribcage, and she motions in an irritated fashion toward the front of the room with a frown. Mr. Remy is giving directions. I must have dozed off.

"Before lunch, you're in for a treat: our exciting Kick-Off-The-Year pep assembly! When the bell rings, we'll make our way to the gym. Don't forget your art supplies list when you leave. We'll start our drawing unit next week!" Mr. Remy's hands speak volumes, opening and closing to the rhythm of his voice like he's shaping invisible clay.

Assembly. A gathering? How many people exactly? Or more specifically, how many boys? My breath catches. Too many, no doubt... as many as can be shoved in the tin can of a gymnasium. Lots and lots of people, with no space to hide. I gaze at Lyla, but she's got her phone back in her lap, like it's not the end of the world and reality hasn't crumbled around us. *Breathe,* the faint rational voice in my head reminds me. But I can't.

I'm a passenger on the express train to Anxiety City.

My throat closes up and panic takes total control for the first time in a long time.

Wheezing and clutching at my neck with both hands, I beg the oxygen to flow into my constricted lungs. Bass drum heartbeats bang louder and louder in my ears. My vision turns black at the edges, like a dying light bulb on the edge of the universe. *SMACK*! I collide, hard, with the classroom floor as consciousness abandons me.

Chapter 9

GENTLE STRING MUSIC INTERRUPTS the emptiness and rouses me, paired with a hint of fresh cut grass and antiseptic wipes. I automatically scrunch my nose. My head pounds against the back of my eyelids like a hammer. *Ouch, ouch, ouch.* I'm lying on my back, and there's soft fabric brushing against my exposed arms. A blanket? Blinking awake, I push myself upright, only for the room to violently spin. My stomach twists into a knot and I retch off the side of the bed. Nothing comes up.

I've woken in an unfamiliar office, framed by stark white walls supporting locked metal cabinets. My cot and a silver desk are the only furniture that fits into the limited space. A small window opens to the lawn outside, emitting a cool breeze, while the desktop radio plays relaxing guitar music. Holding my head in both hands, I try to remember today's patchwork sequence of events.

Art class with Lyla, an unfinished painting, and then, an announcement. The assembly! Trembling, I recall my panic attack, the chest constriction with black-tinged vision. I must have fainted. A stinging pain along my left side confirms the suspicion. Lifting my shirt, I note a purple bruise swelling above my hip. A quick glance in a small oblong mirror reveals discoloration also blooming along my left cheek. I must have fallen hard.

A tall man in a crisp polo shirt swings open the door, and I fight the instinct to scoot as far back as I can on the cot.

He beams from ear to ear before rolling a cushioned desk chair closer to me and stretching out a gloved hand.

"Hello, Maybelline. Good to meet you! My name's Mr. Kevin." The man says in a deep baritone.

Tentatively, I grip his fingertips and give a quick shake, while my heart skips round my chest. Rule #2 (no boys) flies out the open window (again). This day just keeps getting better and better.

"I'm the school nurse!" Mr. Kevin announces. "You've had a nasty fall. Can I look more closely at your head?"

He waits for my nod then pulls a small flashlight out of his pocket. Mr. Kevin leans close enough for me to smell his minty toothpaste and shines his little light into both of my eyes. I do my best to stay still even though the anxiety gnaws hungrily at my insides. Tears trickle down my cheeks.

"No concussion, thank goodness! Unfortunately, those bruises will last a while. Just call them your sixth-grade battle scars. You've got someone waiting to see you." Mr. Kevin gives me a thumbs up and exits the room. Aunt Julie immediately enters, wringing her hands together like she's trying to strangle the life out of her purse strap.

"Oh, Maybe!" She throws her arms tight around me and I flinch. Aunt Julie retreats. "I'm sorry, I wasn't thinking! You poor thing." She brushes a thumb against my temple and down my jawline. More baby tears squeeze from my eyes, but mostly from embarrassment.

A quick knock at the door and Mr. Kevin reappears.

"The school guidance counselor, Mrs. Nightingale, would like to chat with you before you head home." Mr. Kevin crouches down to eye level and meets my gaze with suspiciously genuine concern. "Please rest up and return to school real soon."

Aunt Julie escorts me out of the office, hands tense atop my shoulders. Almost too tight, but I let her squeeze away. She steers me down the hall to another small office. A petite woman with white-blonde hair pulled back in a loose bun waves at us from behind a tidy wooden desk.

The hard-backed leather chairs squeak when we sit down. Mrs. Nightingale shakes Aunt Julie's hand before bustling behind her desk and retrieving a china teapot from a desktop warmer. She pours each of us a cup of steaming tea, ripe with the sweet smell of blueberries, and settles in behind her desk.

"I'm so pleased to meet you both and officially welcome you to Harper Lee Middle School!" Mrs. Nightingale flashes a glistening grin and takes a tiny sip of her tea. Aunt Julie shifts in her seat and reaches for the delicate teacup and places it in her lap. I clasp my hands tight like two pieces of metal soldered together. Exhaustion rests heavy on my eyelids, and all I want is to curl up for a nap. Mrs. Nightingale's beaming smile has other plans.

"Maybelline, you are one smart cookie. I was impressed with your homeschool grades. Simply phenomenal!" She leans closer, as if conspiring, and I spy a sprinkling of freckles scattered across her cheeks. I count the flecks so I don't have to look her in the eye. My cheeks burn hot, and I swallow the enormous lump in my throat. That giant panic attack elephant in the room tramples all over my brain, and I wish I could turn invisible, or blend in like a chameleon.

"Now then, we want to help any way we can with your adjustment to a new school! Switching from homeschool to public school is a huge step, and you've shown such courage thus far." Mrs. Nightingale gives me a wink, eyelashes fluttering like feathers in flight. I'm grateful she hasn't mentioned my fainting spell.

"I'd like you to take a day at home to decompress and return to school on Wednesday, if possible. You can meet in my office each morning in place of your homeroom. I know I'm much less exciting than hanging out with your peers, but how does that sound at least to start?" An almost imperceptible nod from me and she turns her attention to Aunt Julie. Phew. Some of the pressure in my chest diminishes and I sink back in my chair to release a thin breath.

"I'd love to have Maybelline's therapist's contact information. If it's all right, can you jot it down on this form and sign off on the release of information? Together, we'll make an excellent team to tackle this transition."

She hands Aunt Julie a clipboard and pen. Aunt Julie's hand shakes as she writes. Her cursive stretches like a rubber band close to breaking. Guilt chomps at my stomach. I bite the inside of my cheek and force my eyes closed to focus on breathing.

Aunt Julie's warm hand slips into mine. "We appreciate your kindness! If there's some way Mars or I can help, we'll do whatever we can. Maybelline has a bright future, and we want to be as supportive as possible." Aunt Julie tugs my hand—hint, hint—and I have to open my eyes to stand up. With clunky feet, I sway back and forth for a second, suddenly dizzy, and Aunt Julie returns her hands to my shoulders. She guides me to the office door and Mrs. Nightingale follows us out into the hall, heels tapping a cheerful rhythm against the tile. The grown-ups share a look they think I don't see, and Aunt Julie leads me out of the school.

Mama's angry voice chimes in my inner ear. *Failure, failure, failure. My daughter, the scaredy-cat introvert.*

Well, Mama, I'm still just me.

Chapter 10

I'M SURPRISED THAT WE don't get pulled over with Aunt Julie's frantic driving. She pumps the gas a little too hard at each green light, and I white-knuckle the seat cushion for dear life. Any minute flashing lights will appear behind us, I'm sure of it. Can they take us to jail for speeding? I imagine a sterile metal cell would be oddly similar to my brain cage. Trapped and at the mercy of outside forces, no real self-control. Aunt Julie takes a hill too fast, and I float out of the seat a second before forcefully plunking myself back down.

By the time we pull into the therapist office parking lot, I'm pretty sure I've mangled the car cushions or at least left a permanent imprint of my fingertips against the quilted leather. Aunt Julie vacates the car immediately, closing the door hard enough that the entire vehicle tremors. I calmly unbuckle my seatbelt and exit, proof that anxiety can be extremely unpredictable. Despite my aunt's obvious concern, after leaving the school my entire body finally relaxed. I can actually breathe again: full, deep, satisfying breaths.

Aunt Julie hovers around me, straightening my hair and feeling my forehead like I've caught some kind of fever. Once she deems me stable, we wordlessly hustle into the office, but Miss Mendoza's door is shut and the white noise machine whirrs at a steady thrum. Aunt Julie still won't speak, instead pacing across the broad floorboards with pent-up energy. Could my silence actually be contagious? She notices me watching and stops mid-step to perch rigidly on the waiting room couch.

At long last, Miss Mendoza's door swings open. Aunt Julie is up like a shot, pulling at my sleeve while a slouchy middle-aged man leaves. Miss Mendoza's floral blouse reminds me of the library garden in springtime, and instantly I wish I was curled up with a book far away from this whole mess. The longing floods through me as an itch I can't scratch.

"Maybelline! Wonderful to see you!" Miss Mendoza beams at me while Aunt Julie wobbles where she stands.

"Thank you for meeting with her on such short notice," my aunt whispers.

"I'm always happy to spend some quality time with Maybelline. Come on in and we'll have a chat." Miss Mendoza beckons with a manicured hand; I step forward, but Aunt Julie does too. She's back to wringing the life out of her purse strap.

"I'd love to chat with Maybelline to start, and then we can reconvene before the end of the session." Once I cross the threshold, Miss Mendoza shuts the door while Aunt Julie forlornly stays put, much like a lost puppy.

A new candle burns bright on the end table closest to the couch: eucalyptus. The earthy, twinkling scent washes over me, soothing as a warm bath. Biting my thumbnail, I wait on the fluffy couch for Miss Mendoza to finish scribbling on her notepad.

"Let's discuss your first day of middle school. I know the promise of exposure increased your anxiety during our last few sessions. I want you to rate your anxiety level using your fingers, one being the least and ten being the most." Miss Mendoza glances at her notepad. "Sound good?"

I hover my hands above my lap in response, self-conscious of my fingernails, chewed down to nubs.

"How anxious did you feel at the end of our previous session?"

I think for a second and hold up five fingers. Middle of the road.

"How about shopping for your school supplies?"

Eight fingers. The stomachache from shopping lasted all night.

"What about this morning, before heading to school?"

I consider taking off my socks to use my toes, but then

just hold up the full ten fingers. My hair falls in front of my face when I bow my head, cheeks flush with embarrassment. "Oh, Maybe. The exposure process is very difficult, and I am so proud of you for tackling it today even though you were scared." Miss Mendoza's voice is sweet as honey and soothes the sharp sting in my heart. "I think what's important now is to fill your toolbox with coping skills to make the anxiety more manageable as you transition to public school."

Miss Mendoza passes me the notepad and pen. "Can you jot down what you remember from school? What experiences caused the greatest anxiety? It's okay if you don't know for sure. Just write a few ideas and we'll go from there." Her hand lingers on top of mine, a soft reminder that she's got my back. She's not judging me. My shoulders relax a little more, and I meticulously start my notes.

When I peek back at the clock, I'm shocked to see that fifteen minutes have disappeared. I've only got four details on the notepad. Then again, I spent a fair amount of time decoding the day's events while repetitively clicking my pen. I should ask Aunt Julie to buy more clicky pens, though I'd probably drive Lyla batty. Straightening, I return the notepad to Miss Mendoza.

Miss Mendoza smiles her brilliant smile. "Let's see what we're working with."

Triggers

> *Boy classmate (Oliver?)*
>
> *Messy writing*
>
> *Unfinished painting*
>
> *Crowded assembly*

"Excellent job, Maybe! The first step to conquering a fear is self-awareness. Now we can build some coping strategies! But first, let's meditate a bit, then we'll ask your aunt to join in."

I lie down on the couch, and we practice timing my breaths to music. A tranquil sensation drifts through my limbs and, sinking further into the cushions, I notice Miss

Mendoza has a collection of decals stuck to the ceiling. How have I not seen these before? Butterflies, bees, ladybugs, and dragonflies flit across the textured drywall in a playful parade. I trace their paths with my mind as I breathe in and out, in and out. Oxygen, a medicine for my tired body.

By some miracle, my endless brain loops transform into a gentle dance, keeping pace with the lazy insects above. Anxiety quiets and the only remaining sound is the chimes of music leading my exercise. I stifle a grateful giggle and keep breathing.

Chapter 11

WE LEAVE THE OFFICE with a detailed plan in place: try school again, but with a ton of anxiety-fighting weapons in my arsenal. Miss Mendoza gave me a smiley face stress ball to squeeze when I'm triggered. She also said she would talk with Mrs. Nightingale about using her office as a "safe spot" for when I get too anxious to stay in class. I even concocted my own worthwhile idea… using relaxing music to help focus my breathing. Aunt Julie said she'll speak to the principal about permission to carry headphones with me. Public school still scares me, but at least now I'll have some armor.

While the adults chat after therapy, I wander outside and home in on a desperate chirping from the tree out front. A baby bird has fallen from the nest into the twiggy undergrowth and screeches for its Mama. The strings attached to my heart tug me forward into action. I'm careful to lift the wriggling chick using a tissue I've got in my pocket. The baby quiets as soon as it's safe in the nest, and I catch sight of a little blemish on its tummy. A tuft of white feathers, in the shape of a star. Hopefully that's a good omen. At the very least, I'm proud I was able to help. So happy and calm, in fact, that I manage to take a short nap on the drive home.

Tuesday consists of gathering supplies and sparring with the dread that on Wednesday I'll be back inside the belly of Harper Lee Middle School. Uncle Mars keeps me company as I write in my journal. I lose myself in cursive while he tinkers with a broken laptop. His enthusiastic humming is the perfect soundtrack to calm my nerves. Aunt Julie had to go back to work, though she wanted to stay home and trail me to make sure I'm okay. I insisted the orthodontist's office needed her more than me, and at last she gave in. She only called Uncle Mars to check on me about a dozen times. I know I'm broken, but it's not like my panic attacks are anything new.

Curled on the dining bench with the journal in my lap, I focus on the task at hand: brainstorming cool stories for my future writing career. If I wasn't convinced before about being an author, the events of the last couple days sealed the deal. As a writer, I can stay home and create any world I want, without pesky outside distractions stealing my breath or challenging my grasp on reality. I'm going to make my own reality through books.

I inhale a sweet whiff of the library from the journal's cover and chew on the tip of my pencil's eraser. My new story idea list isn't promising yet, but I've got a start: glow-in-the-dark bugs in a garden at night, a black cat that can slink through solid walls like a specter, a shifting shadow that can transform into any fear, and a moody dark-haired girl who always wears a judgmental scowl. Even though the shadow would be the obvious choice, I think the girl will be the villain, judging by how she makes me ache for vengeance. But we'll see.

My creative process slams to a halt when the front door flies open and Lucy comes tumbling into the kitchen, lunch bag in one hand and folder in the other. The wind has swept her hair into a tangle, and her little eyes sparkle with excitement.

"Dad, Dad, Dad! Look what I made at school!" Lucy plucks a sheet of paper from her folder, revealing a crayon drawing of her family. She's got Uncle Mars as the biggest figure, with Aunt Julie right beside him. Lyla's arms are crossed holding a tiny rectangle, presumably a cell phone. In the picture, Lucy has a bright yellow dress, and I creep closer to examine the character with crimped blonde hair (me). Almost everyone in the picture, even Lyla, wears a goofy smile—except for me. I'm shocked when the details of my character come into focus. The nasty frown on doodle-me stretches from cheek to cheek in a dark slash of black crayon. Lucy even drew a little storm cloud above my head. Uncle Mars scoops Lucy up with one hand and relieves her of the paper, eyeing me for a reaction. I fight to keep my expression neutral even though a giant lump settles painfully in my throat. I won't cry. Not over a stupid drawing.

"Luce, how come you've got a dog in the corner?" Uncle Mars puzzles, tilting her picture at a wide angle away from me.

"That's Barkley! He's my Christmas present. I'm gonna send Santa some cookies with my letter this year to make sure I'm on the nice list." Lucy dumps her lunchbox on the counter and rifles through the pantry, stuffing a sugar cookie in her mouth for good measure.

"Sweetie, that's called bribery. Being a good friend is the best way to get on the nice list!" Uncle Mars starts to hang Lucy's picture on the fridge but changes his mind. "I'll set this by the door so Mom can see it when she gets home!" he calls as he heads out of the kitchen toward the entryway.

Smooth, Uncle Mars. Smooth.

Lucy retrieves another cookie from the pantry and eyes the goodie, her little brows creasing. After a long moment, she breaks the treat in half and extends a portion to me. Crumbs litter the floor like sand on a beach. Barkley would have a field day.

"Sharing is caring!" Lucy exclaims with a full mouth.

I try to smile, but the drawing prowls in the back of my mind, weighing me down. I retreat to the dining bench and nibble on my cookie.

"Cookie starts with C, Maybe! C sounds like a cough!" Lucy gives a dramatic hack and I shield my face from incoming splatter.

Uncle Mars returns and claps his hands. "Okay, Lucy, what's the homework damage today?"

Lucy shimmies to her backpack and pulls out a lined notebook. With a skip, she joins me at the table and opens the spiral to a blank page.

"I've got to write my spelling words. Unicorn pencil, don't fail me now!"

Before Lucy can rope me into her lesson, I drift out of the kitchen and up to my room. My loops are full throttle and way too fast to concentrate on my stories. Lucy's drawing plays over and over on a screen in my brain like a recurring nightmare.

Am I so different from the rest of my family? Do they really think I'm never happy? Does everyone who knows me just pretend to like having me around?

Nervous energy courses through my body in an electric wave.

Why have I let my fear define me?

I clasp my stress ball in one hand and dig my nails into the soft surface, blinking away tears. I don't want to be the storm cloud on everyone's otherwise sunny day.

Pulling out the assignment from therapy, I add a new item to my wishlist of changes. Squishing the stress ball makes cursive difficult, but I need somewhere to release the nervous energy. If I bottle the tension inside me, I may explode. My stomach flops with a worried gurgle.

I add a star to make my new entry a top priority.

Things I'd like to change:

Going to middle school

Mama

★ *Lucy's drawing*

Things I'd like to stay the same:

The library

Chapter 12

HALL PASS

WEDNESDAY ARRIVES WITH AUTUMN hot on its heels. Almost overnight, the leaves on the neighborhood trees tinge with vibrant fall colors, reminding me of last year when Lyla colored the tips of her hair a bright orange. A breeze trickles through the cracked open windows of the SUV and rustles my hair. Although my new purple sweater from Aunt Julie swaddles me in fuzzy warmth, an unnatural chill has burrowed deep into my bones. I shiver as we drive to the school, grappling with my stress ball and wishing it was a clicky pen. Lyla rests against the headrest, eyes closed as if she's sleeping, but the uptempo notes resonating from her headphones tell a different story. She is calm, cool, collected—emotionally, we are polar opposites.

To Miss Mendoza's credit, my anxiety has waned the tiniest bit in comparison to Monday. Nine fingers up instead of ten. I still don't think exposure is a good idea, but I can't deny I'm curious how school will go over the next week—or even month. Will it actually be easier? Is that possible?

Aunt Julie practically shoveled eggs and toast into my mouth this morning, and the full belly anchors me as we pull parallel to the school sidewalk. Lyla mumbles goodbye, hops to the pavement and rushes to join her friends. She must be grateful babysitting duty is over 'cause the smile on her face is bigger than the Cheshire cat's. Heat floods my face and I bite the inside of my cheek.

"I've got a meeting with the principal in a half hour to talk about your... plan. Remember, you can visit Mrs. Nightingale any time, and I'm only a phone call away." Aunt Julie helps me out of the car and tucks a wisp of hair behind my ear, studying my face. The school's seen more of Aunt Julie than her orthodontist office has this week, and her absence from work is my fault. She hugs me, but Mama's voice whispers in my head, *You're so needy.* I break from the hug and force myself to walk into the school, careful not to turn back and show how weak I've gone in the knees. Deep breaths. I entered Harper Lee Middle School before, and the experience didn't kill me—only mortified me in front of my classmates.

Winding through the halls toward Mrs. Nightingale's office, a red-haired girl from homeroom flashes her nail polish at a group of friends and three boys in baseball jerseys congregate at the water fountain. I steer clear of the pack and lose myself in the hustle and bustle of the school morning.

The rustle of papers, high-pitched children's laughter, and metallic bangs from slammed locker doors swell around me. I want to cover my ears, but instead I squeeze my stress ball and imagine I'm walking through the pages of a book about middle school and the students are characters in the story. My breath comes easier as my interest piques. I wonder what everyone's backstory could be. Suddenly, the hallway transforms into a treasure trove of information for my future books. I reach to retrieve my notebook to record the wave of ideas, but to my great surprise, I'm already standing outside of Mrs. Nightingale's office. Talk about teleportation. Reluctantly, I shoulder into the office and shut her door behind me. The school goings-on mute to a dull thrum, like someone turned down the volume on a radio. It seems smaller, more manageable already.

When I shuffle in, Mrs. Nightingale looks up from her laptop and breaks into a stunning thousand-watt smile. "Maybelline, good morning! Come on in and take a seat! I'm thrilled you're back at school. How are you feeling?"

I give her a thumbs up, but squeeze the smiley face a little tighter behind my back. Personal attention isn't my favorite pastime.

"Good, good," Mrs. Nightingale mumbles as she clicks a few keys on her laptop. "I've emailed with Miss Mendoza and I'm impressed by the plan you've set up for school. You really are full of smart ideas, Maybelline."

I blush and fiddle with the zipper on my backpack, keeping my eyes trained on the paisley rug.

"I took the liberty of making you a special pass to use if you get overwhelmed in class." Mrs. Nightingale opens the top drawer of her desk to withdraw a laminated notecard. She's inscribed **HALL PASS** in big bold letters on the front and written her signature at the bottom. The cursive may be small and compact, but I'm hypnotized by the accuracy of her swirls. Mrs. Nightingale's signature looks like she typed it on the computer. By comparison, my writing is a total mess. Jealousy tingles in my gut.

"Take a few minutes now to journal about this morning," Mrs. Nightingale instructs. "Remember to use your breathing to help you relax. Once the bell rings, you can head to your first period." She refocuses on her computer, and I throw myself into my library journal. We exist in blissful silence for the remainder of homeroom, and by some miracle my pulse falls into a steady, even rhythm.

The rest of my day isn't perfect, but I'd call the improvement nothing short of a miracle. With each class transition, I become better adjusted to the new routine. With each trill of the bell and wave of students between classes my heartbeat goes manic, but then it slows once I'm seated in the back of the next classroom and the teacher begins the daily lesson. I mind my own business and keep my head down while I work. The other students don't interact with me at all—a welcome surprise—and by the final class I'm riding an incredible high at having survived an entire day of school. All by myself. Who'd have thunk? Coincidentally enough, English with Ms. Bennet is last on the timetable. If I attended homeroom, this room would be the bookends to my schedule. I love how balanced that feels.

I sit in the same seat as homeroom on Monday, but gratefully rejoice that Lyla is no longer next to me with her judgmental stare. Ms. Bennet talks about required reading for the year and distributes the list of books we'll cover. My happiness soars through the roof at the mention of assigned reading. Perhaps one day my own books will be taught in schools around the country. I'll help other kids like me!

Ten minutes to the final bell, and a beep reverberates

from the loudspeaker.

"Maybelline Reed, report to the office. Maybelline Reed, please report to the office," the secretary drones.

"Ooooooooooh," the class exclaims. Twenty-five pairs of eyes swivel in unison to ogle me. My heart plummets like a heavy stone and I freeze, stiff in my seat. There's only one reason I can think of for being called to the office—a summons by the principal. I should have known the comfortable feeling wouldn't last. It never does. My brain swirls ominously in dreadful loops as I stagger to the door and into the hallway, clutching my backpack in front of me like a shield. Every step feels as if I'm dragging my feet through wet concrete. Some of the pressure in my head releases when I get out of view of the kids but promptly returns as I worry about why the principal would want to see me. Aunt Julie was going to talk to him... so the summons could be related to their meeting. Mama whispers maliciously in my inner ear, *Did you break the rules, Maybelline? Why can't you just listen?* I rack my brain for mistakes I may have made, but come up blank. With each step closer to the office, my breathing becomes shallower, until all I can do is gasp for air.

The administrative assistant barely looks up when I arrive. She chatters on the phone with someone she calls "Ma'am" about "PTO." Sinking into a scratchy office chair, my sudden lightheadedness makes the room swim. The fluorescent lights hum a terrible droning chant, and I close my eyes to massage my temples, all the while listening for the principal's wooden door to open.

One drawn out creak moments later, and I know it's time. Tears gather at the edge of my vision, and I stay bent over, clenching my fingers on my smiley face ball so hard it glowers at me.

"Maybelline, honey, come on in."

Mrs. Nightingale?

She holds out a hand and I rise without clasping it, anxious she'll be able to feel me trembling. Where's the principal? Is he waiting in Mrs. Nightingale's office? Confused, I trail behind the guidance counselor in a half-numb fog.

We enter her office space. Slouched in one of Mrs. Nightingale's leather chairs is none other than that curly-haired boy from homeroom. I stop dead, blinking an SOS in

Morse code.

"Maybelline Reed, meet Oliver Grant."

Oliver crosses his arms across his chest without turning around and kicks at a lump in the carpet.

That heavy stone jostles around in my stomach as my brain kicks into catastrophe mode. For what logical reason might Mrs. Nightingale need to talk to both of us?

Gulp. Definitely nothing good.

WELCOME, LADIES AND GENTLEMAN, to the most terrifying ride on Earth. In Maybelline Reed's mind, you'll experience death-defying drops, stops, twists, and turns as thoughts rampage out of control in violent loop-de-loops. Take caution not to cling too tightly to reality. Side-effects may include a racing pulse, sweaty palms, crippling panic, and an uncontrollable urge to puke. Ummmm, how about all of the above?

Mrs. Nightingale's office may as well be the blazing surface of the sun. It's gotten so stinking hot. Fidgeting in my chair, a pool of sweat gathers at the base of my spine and I clench my jaw to anchor myself to the present. I refuse to pass out again. My temples throb with an emerging headache, but I force myself to sit patiently while Mrs. Nightingale fetches each of us a cup of tea. Oliver slouches in the chair next to me, oblivious to my rising tension. Typical boy.

"Now, you're both probably wondering why I've dragged you to the office," Mrs. Nightingale chirps with a giggle. She places a teacup in front of each of us. I leave mine alone, afraid my shaking will break the delicate porcelain. The phantom rattle haunts me without even touching it.

A nervous laugh rises in my throat and releases with a croak. Oliver stays silent, hands thrust in his hoodie pocket. He's watching his teacup closely, as if expecting it to perform a magic trick.

How about we make Maybelline disappear? I silently plead.

Mrs. Nightingale continues, chipper as ever.

"Your class schedules this year are perfectly synced, so I've had a thought that might benefit you both. Oliver, your... social confidence could be helpful for Maybelline. And Maybelline, your studious mentality would certainly broaden Oliver's academic horizons."

Oliver breaks his staring contest with the cup to glare at Mrs. Nightingale. I'm trying to keep my teeth from chattering as she drops the bomb.

"How would you like to team up for the school year? Oliver, you can help Maybelline get acclimated to public school, and she can tutor you in your more challenging subjects." Mrs. Nightingale beams from ear to ear as if she's solved some complicated equation.

"I'm not stupid," Oliver growls.

"Oh dear, not at all. But if we're being honest with each other, your grades are in a tough spot. The last couple years have put you a little behind, and I think this arrangement could help you get back on track." Mrs. Nightingale reaches out a hand to Oliver, but he merely shrugs and leans back further in his chair.

I've gone numb throughout my insides, which I suppose is better than having a full on panic attack in the confines of Mrs. Nightingale's office. My brain loops spin faster and faster, trying to compute how I'll survive regular interaction with Oliver, and now my headache straight up pounds against my skull like a hammer. The day had been going so well. Massaging the back of my neck and avoiding Mrs. Nightingale's gaze, I retreat further into my shell.

She notices.

"Maybelline, I wouldn't ask anything of you that I don't think you can handle," she whispers soft and comforting. I give an obligatory nod, so she'll let me be.

"Oh, and that reminds me! Maybelline, I've heard through the grapevine that you enjoy writing. I've got some exciting news!" Mrs. Nightingale says brightly. "Ms. Bennet plans to start a school paper this year. How would you and Oliver like to be involved?"

Some of the pressure lifts from my shoulders and I straighten in my chair. A school paper? I'd write articles that people would actually read? It'd be like I'm talking to them without having to open my mouth. Perhaps Mama would even see one of my articles and reach out to let me know. A surge of joy rushes through me, and I nod more vigorously.

"Oliver, once again, you and Maybelline will act as a team for the paper. It will be a good opportunity for you both to grow, academically and socially. If you actively participate, we'll consider your contributions as extra credit toward your grades."

I expect Oliver to show some gratitude, but...

"So, you're paying me off?" he replies, monotone.

Mrs. Nightingale purses her lips, but continues. "Consider it an opportunity to put the past behind you."

At that, Oliver hangs his head low and fiddles with his hoodie strings although he can't hide the way his frown deepens at the corners. Mrs. Nightingale touched a nerve. I feel a little sorry for him, even if he's a boy.

Mrs. Nightingale claps her hands together and rises from her chair, alight with excitement.

"Why don't you two shake on it to seal the deal?" She watches us expectantly, and I sense Oliver shift in his seat to face me. I can be brave, I think. I just got through an entire school day.

Forcing a deep breath in and out, I don't give myself time to mull, instead pivoting in my chair and extending my trembling hand. *Do it for the paper. Do it for the future. Do it for Mama.* Oliver doesn't hesitate even a second. I cover most of my hand with my sleeve, but our skin brushes fingertip to fingertip. He grasps my palm gently for a quick shake, then lets it fall. The warmth lingers in my fingers, and I flex them with surprise. By the time I look up again, he's gathered his backpack and vanished out the door. Mrs. Nightingale smiles at me all the while.

"I'm proud of you, Maybelline," she says when I stand up. I'm puzzled that the world hasn't imploded in light of my broken rules. At the door, I wave goodbye with a shy smile. Although the loops whirl in the back of my brain, one reassuring thought emerges from the mess. A quiet, hopeful inner voice I haven't heard in I don't know how long: mine.

I'm proud of me too.

Chapter 14

Uncle Mars waves from his bright red Jeep. The car's backseat is empty. Lyla must have picked the bus. I don't mind; better for me. I jump onto the quilted leather backseat and tension melts from my shoulders as Uncle Mars pulls away from the school.

"Hey, kiddo. How was your day?" he asks as Harper Lee Middle School shrinks to a speck behind us. I give him a distracted thumbs up as I burrow through my backpack, struck by sudden inspiration. At last my fingers wrap around my most recent library book, *The Unicorn Chronicles* by Bruce Coville, which will be due by the end of the week.

Flourishing the book toward Uncle Mars, I gesture emphatically at the sticker on the front cover that reads "Property of Salem Public Library." Uncle Mars takes the hint with a chuckle, turning right at the nearest traffic circle.

"They should put you on the library payroll, Maybe. You probably know those shelves better than anybody else." He steers into the tiny parking lot alongside my favorite building in the world. "You okay walking home or do you want me to wait?"

I almost roll my eyes but for the life of me would never want to channel my inner Lyla, and especially not at Uncle Mars, so instead I bound out of the car and cheerfully wave goodbye to him. The rest of the lot lies deserted, but that's how I like it. *Creak, creak, creak* up the porch steps and I walk into the magical, musty smell of my home away from home. Fishing a penny out of my pocket, I flip it into the bucket as I pass, walking on while I cast my wish.

I wish I was a famous author. My heart sings.

The library interior seems extra dark today, and I home in on a few dead lightbulbs scattered throughout the ceiling lights. Warily, I hesitate and scan the room for Mr. Campbell to appear from behind the shelves with a ladder, but the library rests quieter than a pin drop. I proceed to the return counter.

Cuddles' little paws are tucked beneath his body while he lies immobile atop the front desk like a fuzzy loaf of bread. He greets me with an emotionless stare. Mrs. Campbell must be in the back room. I ding the little silver bell on the counter and its chime reverberates loud and clear through the echoey space. I want to be sure Mrs. Campbell knows I returned my book. Normally, Cuddles keeps his distance, but I must be lucky today. While I wait, I stroke the silky fur along his back, and he leans into my hand.

Just as the bell's vibration fades, Mrs. Campbell emerges from a door behind the desk and hustles to help me. But right away, I notice how her cheeks are red and puffy, and her eyes droop. She clasps a crinkled handkerchief tightly in her palm. Upon recognizing me, her expression brightens like a new lightbulb.

"Maybelline, my dear! Sorry to keep you waiting!" Her voice cracks and she clears her throat before continuing. "To what do I owe this pleasure?"

I softly place my book on the counter and Mrs. Campbell wipes her nose with her kerchief before tucking the evidence away in her dress pocket. She scans the barcode on the inside cover and adds the book to a wheeled cart behind the desk. I spot a few of my recent returns in the stack. Weird. Mrs. Campbell re-shelves books like clockwork. She told me herself she doesn't like patrons missing out on a book that hasn't been replaced.

"Take your time, dear. It's nice to have company. Been quiet around here since Mr. Campbell has been testing out retirement." Mrs. Campbell doesn't look me in the eye. That's a surefire way to tell a grown-up is lying... I saw it from Mama often enough.

Scrunching my brow, I watch Mrs. Campbell out of the corner of my eye while I meander through the shelves to the computers. Every so often she sniffles. Cuddles relocates to her lap and sits pressing up against her.

I can't shake the feeling that something's wrong. Usually, the library soothes my anxiety, but today the back of my neck prickles a warning, and I shiver. Trying to ignore my negative gut instinct, I boot up the computer and bury myself in writing my email. I can't help but swivel occasionally to peer through the bookshelves to check on Mrs. Campbell. I'm distracted enough that the big fat 0 for new emails in my inbox doesn't so much as make me blink.

Dear Mama,

I started my new adventure! Somehow, middle school is exactly what I expected and completely different, all at the same time. There are too many kids, especially boys, but I'm learning a lot already.

I've decided to be a writer when I grow up. You always told the best stories, so I bet I'll be really good at it. Harper Lee's guidance counselor asked me to join the school paper. If you send me your address, I can mail you a copy. Otherwise, I'm sure they'll put a version online and I can email it to you.

Anyway, I miss you a bunch and can't wait to hear from you. Fingers crossed that school gets easier. I'm gonna try my best to fit in.

Love,
Maybelline

I tap send and shut down the computer. Skipping to the children's section, I make good use of the paper and crayons on one of the miniature tables. My cursive is far from perfect because I'm writing fast, but the words come so quickly that I let my loops deal with it.

Once there was a library
That truly meant the world to me
It had the best books
And great reading nooks

Where I let my imagination run free.

For good measure, I doodle a little picture of Cuddles in the corner to be sure Mrs. Campbell knows I mean Salem Public Library. Then I fold the poem into a tiny paper square and hustle over to the bookshelves. I grab the last book on the C shelf without even looking at the cover. I want to get back to the front desk to give Mrs. Campbell my poem.

Cuddles reclines comfortably on her lap as I approach, and Mrs. Campbell has her face in her hands like her head weighs a hundred pounds. She runs shaky fingers through her hair and reaches out for my book selection. Upon noticing the cover, her entire face brightens with a nostalgic smile.

"*Walk Two Moons* by Sharon Creech. Maybe, you're in for a real treat. This has got to be one of my most favorite books." Mrs. Campbell licks her fingertip to flip through the pages, reminiscing. I shift from foot to foot and set the little paper square on top of the counter.

"What's this, honey?" Mrs. Campbell unfolds the paper, and her eyes skim slowly across the lines of cursive. With each word read, she smiles a little bigger. "Maybelline, you've got a special way with words and this poem couldn't have come at a better time. I'm honored."

She cradles the paper close to her heart and walks around the desk. "Can I give you a hug, dear?"

I nod my consent and she wraps me up in a warm embrace. Her hair smells of mothballs and coconut, but the hug feels as natural as if she were my grandmother. When she draws away, my pride vanishes as I notice the glisten of fresh tears streaming down her cheeks. Now I'm the one who can't meet her eyes. The poem was supposed to help, but she's still sad. Heat washes over my face and the tips of my ears. Disappointed, I scoop up *Walk Two Moons* and make a speedy retreat out the front door without looking back. Mrs. Campbell calls goodbye, but she stutters in her fragile state. My heart sinks.

Books have never failed to improve my mood, but my poem just made things worse. Shouldering my backpack and hurrying down the sidewalk toward home, I freefall into my all too regular endless loops of anxiety.

What if the kids on the paper laugh at me because I can't write well?
What if Mrs. Bennet kicks me out?
Do I have anything important to say?
What if I'm not meant to be a writer?
Do my words even matter?

Chapter 15

THURSDAY MORNING SCIENCE CLASS gave me the shakes. Literally.

Mrs. Quark must have gotten the memo about my new partnership because as soon as I enter the classroom, she directs me to a seating chart where I'm paired with Oliver at one of the worktables. He's already perched on his metal stool, but he's got his head on the countertop. Is he napping? My stomach flip flops when I sit next to him, and I fight the urge to scoot the stool as far away as reasonably possible. *Breathe*, I remind myself, but my lungs have a mind of their own. I focus on squashing my smiley face ball instead. My gaze stays glued to Mrs. Quark, and, luckily, Oliver doesn't try to start up a conversation with me.

"Welcome back and happy Thursday! Take a moment to acclimate to your new seat, as it will be your assigned spot for the remainder of the year!" Mrs. Quark adjusts the protective goggles on her forehead, and the class groans. Inwardly, I'm screaming. My smiley face pays the price with a series of extra tight chokeholds.

"Today we'll begin our unit on natural disasters! Thursday will always mean science experiments, so you'll be working as a team for this lesson."

A quick peek in my peripheral vision reveals that Oliver has managed to rest his chin upon his hands so he's at least looking at Mrs. Quark. Good. Let him be uninvolved. I'd rather do the science experiment on my own.

"If you've been paying attention to the news, you will have noticed that California has experienced a multitude of earthquakes this summer," she writes *Earthquakes* on the whiteboard, signaling the students to open our spirals and take notes. Oliver doesn't move an inch. The pencil in my palm grounds me, and I throw myself into writing flawless cursive notes. Mrs. Quark talks for about ten minutes about the origin of earthquakes and why certain places experience them more often. I'm surprised to learn that even flat places can have earthquakes; they're just really little ones that go unnoticed. I make a mental note to see if the library has a book on the phenomenon so I can read more about it.

Then, Mrs. Quark calls a student from each table up to the front to collect a bin of materials for our science experiments.

"You'll be working with your partner to make buildings out of craft sticks and marshmallows. You can add however many levels you want, but be aware that we'll test the sturdiness of your buildings at the end of class with our own simulated earthquakes. If you have questions, I'll be making my way around the room. Discuss with your partner what you think might make your buildings more stable." Mrs. Quark presses a green button on her wall timer, and the digital clock begins to tick down from twenty minutes.

A trickle of sweat travels down my back as I unpack the materials onto our table, bracing myself for Oliver to start talking to me. But when our box is empty, we both stew in heavy silence. A clap sounds behind me, and I must jump a foot off my stool.

"Hop to it, dears! The clock is ticking!" Mrs. Quark claps again and immediately I comply, pulling a paper plate close to me so I can cut some holes to insert the craft sticks. Oliver sticks his tongue out at Mrs. Quark when she walks away and pops one of the mini marshmallows in his mouth, chewing extra big. My stomach churns at his closeness to me, but I keep my head down and focus on my work.

"So why don't you talk?" he mutters while drumming his fingers on the table. He picks up a thin wooden craft stick and balances it on his fingertip like a baton.

I meet his eyes for a second and point to the paper plates. He laughs.

"We're just going to wreck them anyways. What's the point?" But he maneuvers his stool a little closer so he can brace the paper plate as I insert four craft sticks and secure them down with marshmallows. He smells of wind and sunshine and fresh cut grass—summertime in the fall. Like he's somehow removed from the rest of us. I suppress the urge to sneeze as my nervous heart runs wild in my chest.

"Besides, earthquakes aren't as bad here as in California. Easy fix: don't move to California." Oliver twists his hoodie string around his forefinger, tight as the loops in my brain. *I'm sitting next to a boy, I'm sitting next to a boy, I'm sitting next to a boy.* This is my new reality. I want to throw up.

Just keep building.

My legs quiver as if an earthquake has kicked off under the school. I move to add a second level to our structure, but Oliver stops me by blocking my hand.

"Wait. We have to strengthen the base first." He retrieves a few more sticks and adds braces at an angle to each of the supporting posts. I can't help but notice how nubby his fingernails are as he assembles the pieces. They're like mine.

Pulling my spiral over, I scrawl a quick question. And by quick question, it probably takes me forever to get the cursive just so. By the time I look back up, Oliver has built an entire second story.

How do you know so much about buildings?

I tap the notebook with my pencil so he notices. He smiles at me when he's done reading.

"So, she does speak," Oliver replies. "My dad's a contractor. Mostly he builds houses, but he's taught me some stuff about how construction works. I used to help him with some projects too. What about your dad?"

I divert my eyes and nibble on my pencil's eraser while I ponder his question. I've never met my actual father. Mama didn't talk about him either. Painfully slow, I jot another note.

My Uncle Mars fixes computers, phones, and stuff like that. We call him a professional tinkerer.

Oliver laughs. "Imagine professional tinkerer as an actual job title."

By this time, our building has a total of three stories. A strange exhilaration captures me, and I'm surprised by how well we've functioned as a team. We both reach for the last marshmallow to fortify the final stick and our hands accidentally brush against each other. The physical contact sends a bolt of anxious energy like static electricity up my arm, snapping my head back. I immediately retract my hand, willing my racing pulse to calm.

Don't ever trust a boy, Maybelline. They'll rip out your heart and stomp on it until it's broken into a thousand pieces. We're better off without them. Mama whispers into my inner ear. What would she think if she could see me now, working on a project with a boy and betraying her advice? I hang my head in shame. At this rate, Mama won't ever trust me again either.

When we've finished our project, Oliver holds up his hand for a high five. I don't respond. I can't. If Mama only knew. Oliver's gaze burns laser hot against my cheek, but thankfully he doesn't say anything. Emotions ripple through me: failure at not controlling my panic, pride at collaborating with a boy, hope that I'll eventually get better, and stabbing regret over losing Mama all rattle together like my insides are cursed with their own seismic waves. My own personal earthquake. Oh goody.

Mrs. Quark's electronic timer blares and the rest of the class quiets. I stare ahead, miserable. One by one, each of the lab teams takes their buildings to the front of the room and Mrs. Quark mimics an earthquake with two boards of wood. She places the structures on top of the boards, then jiggles the top board with gradually increasing force. My classmates erupt into fits of laughter as each craft stick tower inevitably topples.

Oliver and I stand a good arms length away from one another when it's our turn. Mrs. Quark has to shake the wood base extra hard to get our building to fall. I should be happy when she congratulates us on the most stable construction, but really I'm exhausted. Oliver is back to frowning by the time we sit down to wait for the bell. Now I'm the one resting my head on my books, situated away from him so I don't have to witness the hurt written on his face. He has no doubt caught on that I'm not interested in making friends. Mama would never approve of being friends with a boy. I have to break the scary moments into smaller, more manageable segments. Just like Miss Mendoza says.

One class down, six to go.

But when I remember Oliver, my guilty conscience tap dances on my shoulder. This is the way it has to be... so he won't have the chance to hurt me first. After all, Mama knows best.

Right?

THE EUCALYPTUS CANDLE IN Miss Mendoza's office has vanished, replaced with a spiced pumpkin wax jar for fall. The smell takes me back to a Halloween long ago, when Mama surprised me with an ugly blob of a pumpkin.

We named it Silly Pumpkin, and instead of trick-or-treating (because I didn't have a costume), we took our time hollowing out the gourd and carving the funniest imaginable face. Big star-shaped eyes, buck teeth, and a crooked mouth... we even added some pipe cleaner hair, sticking up at all the right angles like it had been struck by lightning.

Excavating Silly Pumpkin got slimy goo on my hands and gloppy pumpkin seeds in my hair, but I didn't care. Mama pulled out a bag of sticky caramels when we were done (her favorite candy, usually stashed in the bottom drawer of her dresser), and we chewed together while watching our jack-o-lantern twinkle upon the surface of our glass kitchen table. The heat of the tiny candle warming my palms, and the comforting pressure of Mama's arm around my shoulders. I remember falling asleep like that, my head pressed against Mama's chest.

When I woke the next morning, she'd moved me to the couch, and Silly Pumpkin was gone. Our kitchen sparkled clean from top to bottom, as if the jack-o-lantern had been a figment of my imagination. Mama was never partial to messes. "Neatness matters, Maybelline," she insisted as she sipped her steamy coffee. Underneath the odor of cleaning supplies and espresso, I caught a sweet lingering whiff of pumpkin. I didn't let her see me cry, retreating instead to my room to mourn Silly Pumpkin. The happy Halloween memory would have to be enough.

Miss Mendoza's tinny chime calls me away from my daydream, beckoning me back to the present. I push upright on the comfy couch, rubbing my eyes with both fists. Saturday should be relaxing, because it's not a school day, but I know Miss Mendoza will want to hear about everything that happened this week. My stomach churns and I cross my arms over my abdomen, hoping some pressure will relieve the rising nausea.

"What's on your mind today, Maybelline? You seem far away." Miss Mendoza passes me a notepad and pen (the non-clicky variety), fixing me with a patient stare.

Mama, I write neatly and pass the notepad back across the void.

"Do you want to talk about it?" Miss Mendoza asks gently, scribbling a note in the folder where she logs my sessions.

I shake my head real slow. The pumpkin wax sputters beside me.

"Okay. We can talk about something else. In fact, I've been meaning to work a new activity into our sessions." Miss Mendoza flashes me a brilliant smile. "What do you say?"

I smile back and inch to the edge of the couch, fully prepared for a change of subject.

"First, I want to congratulate you on completing your first week of middle school. You've been courageous and strong, and I'm proud of you."

Heat floods my face with her generous praise.

Miss Mendoza opens a desk drawer and roots around, looking for something. She pulls out a stack of colored index cards and sets them on the coffee table between us. Pressing play on the nearby stereo, she motions me closer. Peaceful flute notes cascade through the room, setting the mood, and I begin to relax.

"I want us to assess the progress of your feelings with each day spent at school. So, let's begin with some foundation feelings. On each index card, please write an emotion that you've felt within the last seven days."

Fear. Anxiety. Anger. Sadness. Pride. Gratitude. Relief. Curiosity. Shame. Joy.

Ten words, ten cards, just like there are ten letters in my name. Miss Mendoza spreads the cards in a horizontal line across the coffee table then pulls a small basket from the top of her desk and places it in my lap. Within the wicker, I find a collection of vibrant shaped erasers. Dogs, watermelons, baseballs; you name it. I comb through the erasers, waiting for directions.

"We're going to explore each school day and label the emotions you remember, so you have a better idea of which triggers influence your feelings most. So let's start with Monday. Put an eraser on whatever emotions came to life on your first day of school." Miss Mendoza leans back in her chair, and I tap a watermelon eraser to my chin while I think.

Monday: an eraser goes on fear, anxiety, shame. That was the day I fainted in front of my entire class. Definitely not my favorite.

"Great reflection," Miss Mendoza replies. "Now clear the board, and let's continue."

Tuesday: I put the erasers on relief, shame, sadness, anxiety. Gratitude that I spent the day at home. Sadness when I saw Lucy's picture.

Wednesday: erasers on curiosity, pride, anxiety. Everything went well until they called me to the principal's office for the impromptu introduction to Oliver.

Thursday: curiosity, joy, anxiety, sadness, shame each get an eraser. Oliver's rejected expression plays on repeat through my mind's eye. I shudder as I collect the erasers again.

Friday: sadness, sadness, sadness. Three whole erasers. Over Mama, and the silence between me and Oliver when he hadn't done anything wrong. We didn't "talk" the entire day of school. Teamwork destroyed, and I'm totally to blame.

Three erasers on the same emotion and Miss Mendoza's forehead goes all crinkly. She watches me extra close, waiting, and I fiddle with my non-clicky pen.

"You've done really well identifying your emotions, Maybelline. Now we can unpack them a little bit. I know you'd talked about your anxiety peaking with the beginning of school, so Monday and Tuesday make a lot of sense to me. What was the change on Wednesday that switched everything upside down?"

I write a response on the notepad and hand it to her.

The guidance counselor paired me with a boy. She said we could help each other out.

"What's his name?" Miss Mendoza asks.

Oliver.

A stream of butterflies flutters through my stomach as I write it down.

"On Thursday you felt joyful. Was that during school?" I nod and Miss Mendoza perks up. "Can you explain when you felt happy?"

Oliver and I worked on a science experiment. I liked learning about earthquakes, and he had some good suggestions for our project.

Tears well up in my eyes and I brush them away. May as well get it out in the open.

Mama told me never to trust a boy. So I stopped talking to Oliver after the experiment. He got upset.

"And you didn't collaborate any more on Friday?" Miss Mendoza probes.

I shake my head and bite my tongue to distract myself from the intense shame gnawing at my heart.

"Why do you think the silence between you and Oliver made you so sad?" Miss Mendoza whispers. Rather than dwell, I write the honest answer that pops in my head to squelch my annoying worry loops.

Cause he was nice and it seemed like he wanted to be friends. I made him sad.

Miss Mendoza stops the music, which draws my attention away from careful examination of my shoes.

"Maybelline, peer social interaction is new to you. And when a person deals with such strong anxiety, it can put you on the defensive even when it doesn't make sense."

A tear leaks from my eye and Miss Mendoza hands me a Kleenex with a smile.

"Friendship isn't smooth sailing. Even good friends have disagreements once in a while. But if you know you've made a mistake, a friend will forgive you. Just tell Oliver you're sorry you shut him out, and I bet he'll be open to rekindling the friendship."

Apologize to Oliver? Why hadn't I thought of that? The solution feels so simple that Lucy would probably have thought of it. Except, Oliver's a boy and Mama would be appalled if I apologized to a boy.

But Mama's not here, and Oliver is. His feelings matter equally as much as mine.

The promise of forgiveness lights a spark in my heart. The tiny residual warmth reminds me of Silly Pumpkin and his glow. I can do this. Messy mistakes don't have to be permanent.

Now I need to add an eleventh emotion note card to my collection: hope.

Chapter 17

I'M SURE I'LL CHICKEN out, and by chicken out I mean completely avoid the discussion between me and Oliver. Monday morning my anxiety checks in at a solid number eight, which is better than I expected, to be honest. But Oliver doesn't show up, which makes matters worse.

His stool in science sits empty, and I can't help but toss my attention over it every now and again like he may appear out of thin air. A big untouched page stares up from my spiral at the end of class. Notes are impossible when my brain is in hyperdrive.

I tromp into Mr. Kepler's room for math while practicing my breathing but stop in my tracks when I notice Oliver sulking at a desk. Arms stretched across his chest, he rests both feet on the desk in front of him, tapping his toes. I blink a few times, certain I'm hallucinating, but no. He's really there. My muscles tense up like the ratchet strap I've seen Uncle Mars use to move heavy things, and I force myself into the seat next to him as my skin goes cold and clammy. He doesn't even look up.

I can't apologize to a boy. Miss Mendoza has lost her marbles. There's no way Oliver wants to be my friend because *I* wouldn't even want to be my friend. He's better off without me.

Clenching my teeth, I pull out a spiral and pencil, as well as my smiley face squish ball. Mr. Kepler takes attendance and drones on and on about how to calculate probability. There is a 100% chance I'll never have real friends. I can't hear anything clearly over the blood pounding in my ears.

Oliver continues to give me the cold shoulder. Just call me Maybelline the popsicle.

The class releases a collective sigh when Mr. Kepler passes out a pop quiz.

"Are you even allowed to give quizzes during the second week of school?" a boy named Anthony asks. Mr. Kepler fixes him with a serious stare, and Anthony backs down. Pencils scrape across the thin sheets of paper in steady rhythm, and the quiz clears my brain a little. When I peek at Oliver, he sits stationary, not a writing utensil in sight.

Mr. Kepler approaches him when he collects the quizzes.

"Would you like a pencil to complete your work?" Mr. Kepler asks, offering him a sharpened number two. Oliver lifts the blank quiz and brandishes it in the air, and Mr. Kepler's frown deepens like a sad clown. "Very well."

Something's majorly wrong. I rip a page from my notebook and write a cursive peace offering.

Are you okay?

Mr. Kepler's back is turned and once I've taken an enormous, stabilizing breath, I set the note delicately on Oliver's desktop. He reads it but promptly balls up the paper and puts it in his backpack. My anxiety skyrockets. Biting my fingernails, I pack up my belongings to make the switch to art.

Mama's voice whispers sharp criticism: *He hates you.*

****

Mr. Remy never has a bad day. His great booming laughter and toothy smile spread through the students like a positivity contagion. Too bad I'm immune and Oliver's turned to stone.

"As promised, we begin our drawing unit right now!" Mr. Remy exclaims. The class buzzes with excitement as he creates a doodle on the board. His picture says Drawing, but the letters are formed with little pencils. Not cursive, but fascinating nonetheless. I never realized words could be built with images.

Our assignment requires only a pencil and drawing paper. We need to pick a word and choose an image with which to draw the letters. Students chatter happily with their friends while they brainstorm the elements of their projects. I bite my lip and glance at Oliver, but he's already thrown himself into his work. He's using skateboards to write the letter "F." His hand moves confidently, like he's drawn the picture a dozen times before. I want to learn how to do that.

A piece of my brain clicks into place and that spark of hope from therapy flares in my heart. I've got nothing to lose. Worst case scenario, Oliver will squash my drawing and throw it in the trash. But I can't blame him. I find comfort in squishing my smiley face, so I understand the deep-seated need to crush something when upset.

Meticulously (but also speedily because I want to finish in time), a drawing emerges from my imagination. I sketch craft sticks and marshmallows as building blocks for my letters, which makes cursive absolutely impossible because craft sticks don't curve. I can't remember the last time I printed a word, but certainly drawing doesn't count as writing. I cross my fingers and toes and pray that there are no horrible consequences for diverting from cursive. Mama won't find out. She's long gone.

My hand starts to cramp on the last letter, Y, and I flex my fingers for the final push. When I wipe the sweat from my forehead, the graphite on my hand smudges all over. I did it! My drawing is finished. Pride races through me until I'm trembling with excitement.

The craft sticks and marshmallows promise forgiveness, and as soon as Oliver completes his paper and sits up straight, I thrust my drawing in front of his nose. He glares but takes the sheet as I wait nervously to see his reaction, my eyes glued on him. Is it just me or do his shoulders relax? Is that a smirk at the edge of his mouth?

I'M SORRY never felt so good.

Oliver takes his drawing and places it in front of me, a token of friendship that lights the flicker in my heart to a little flame. His skateboards form the word *FREEDOM*, and my heart skips a beat. A dream we're both chasing.

Perhaps we have more in common than I thought.

Chapter 18

SMILEY FACE SQUISH BALL chills at the bottom of my locker for the rest of the school day, and I only lose my breath a handful of times. Since Oliver forgave me, I've turned invincible, like I've donned anxiety-proof armor. I occasionally brush my hand against the picture he's gifted me, hidden away in my library diary, as a reminder that our friendship is real. Each time I envision the skateboard letters, my lips tip up into a smile. The elusive joy emotion card will definitely apply to today.

Students rush through the halls with the final bell, but I take my time, reveling in the low level of anxiety as I pack my necessary textbooks in my backpack and shut my locker with a clang. Is this what it's like to be normal? A steady heartbeat and stable mind, even when chaos courses round me like a river. I shoulder through the entrance doors and into the sunshine, pondering the surreal internal calm.

"Maybelline! Wait up!" Oliver jogs through the doors and up alongside me, backpack clunking into his back. Something heavy rattles around inside. He runs a hand through his curls and catches his breath. A car horn makes us jump in unison.

"Hey, kiddo! Who's your friend?" Uncle Mars rolls down the Jeep's passenger window for a better vantage point. Lucy's darling face mushes against the glass in back, and I can hear her enthusiastic pleading even through the barrier.

"Okay, Luce. Hang tight." Uncle Mars opens her window, too. I'm acutely aware of their closeness to Oliver, and the nerves surge full throttle through my body as air gets vacuumed out of my lungs. Back to my regularly scheduled anxiety program. Fan-tas-tic.

But what's that new underlying feeling, the trigger driving the anxiety? Miss Mendoza always says to pay attention to my triggers. Scalding embarrassment prickles across my cheeks and through my restricted chest like lava. Whether at my family's sudden appearance or being caught next to Oliver, I'm not sure. I fight the urge to hide behind one of the nearby bushes.

"Maybe, guess what! Dad's taking us for ice cream!" Lucy pantomimes licking an ice cream cone.

"Ah yes, ice cream. The only argument strong enough to convince Lucy to skip the bus," Uncle Mars chortles, then clears his throat. "Maybelline, who's your friend?" he repeats.

"Name's Oliver! Oliver Grant." He side-eyes Lucy. She bats her eyelashes at him.

"Want to join us for ice cream, Oliver? It's the Thompson family induction ritual." Uncle Mars motions Oliver closer and lowers his voice to a whisper. "We just really, really like ice cream."

Uncle Mars grins and Oliver laughs, half-heartedly. I shake my head and slash my hand across my throat while his back is turned, but quickly freeze when Oliver pivots his attention to me.

"I was gonna ask for a favor, actually. Do you have some time to help me with math? My dad's gonna kill me for flunking that quiz. Math isn't my favorite," Oliver mumbles, but I can tell he's trying to hide a smirk. My belly warms with a wonderful belonging, tamping out the embarrassment. Someone wants to hang out—with me?

I can't believe I'm about to trade snacking on ice cream for tutoring a boy. Where in the world is Maybelline Reed? Is it possible for change to actually feel good? Once I nod, Oliver readdresses Uncle Mars to ask permission, winning some bonus points from me.

"Where are you heading for the study session?" Uncle Mars asks. I point to my library journal the same time he guesses. "The library? Would you like a ride?"

Oliver takes a few steps back, terror briefly distorting

his face, before his calm, cool and collected mask slides on again. He clenches and unclenches his fists. *Strange.*

"Actually, I've got this," Oliver finally responds, reaching into his stiff backpack and pulling out a bulky folded object. Upon closer inspection, everything makes sense. A foldable skateboard!

Uncle Mars looks doubtful but reads the request written on my face. *Be cool, please!* "Alrighty, then. The library isn't too far. So long as you two stay together and come straight home when you're done. We'll save you some double chocolate soft serve, Maybe."

Oliver unfolds his skateboard with a snap and drops it to the pavement. Driving to the library would have been faster, but since he's the one who asked to hang out, I don't argue the point. I've got nothing against walking. But there's no way I'm getting on that skateboard.

Lucy waves and blows me a kiss as Uncle Mars pulls onto the road, but Oliver doesn't see. He's too busy fiddling with one of the wheels. Thank goodness.

The schoolyard empties as we trek across the sidewalk, and Oliver rolls ahead and banks back to me. He flips the board once or twice, jumping so it swivels mid-air before clunking back to the pavement, feet firmly planted on the black sandpaper surface. Oliver manipulates each jump higher than the last until the ease of motion disappears and his full concentration hinges on his tricks. He glances briefly at me, and I give him a thumbs up. Unfortunately, his maneuver literally goes sideways, board flying one way and Oliver the other, tumbling onto the lawn in an ungraceful splat. No wonder he smells like grass! I rush to help him up, but when he retrieves his skateboard from the curb, he folds it up and stores it again in his backpack. We walk side-by-side as the whoosh of nearby traffic urges us on.

"Have you ever tried skateboarding?" Oliver asks, breathless. He's got a scrape on his wrist, but I don't think he notices.

I reply with a series of quick head shakes and he laughs at me. Or rather, with me, because a giggle sneaks out of my throat. I swallow it down and focus on my breathing.

"What do you like to do for fun?" he asks, hopping onto a nearby parking block and spreading his arms wide for balance. Oliver walks on each parking block like a bridge over a great ravine. I don't know how he isn't exhausted from constant movement. Out-of-school Oliver is totally different than in-school Oliver.

I point to my backpack to answer his question, and he tosses me a skeptical stare.

"Homework? You've got to be kidding me." He scoffs. I plant my feet and put a fist on each hip, matching his attitude before pulling *Walk Two Moons* from the depths of my bag.

"Ohhhhh. Reading," Oliver remarks. "Books are okay, I guess."

My mouth falls open. Understatement of the year!

He laughs.

I hug the novel to my chest and spin in an exuberant twirl. The autumn wind rushes through my hair and engulfs my lungs with the essence of Salem: the earthy smell of farmer-tilled dirt, moisture from clouds heavy with rain, and tangy deliciousness wafting from Mario's Pizza down the street (home of the famous double-decker pizza pie). My eyeballs roll from spinning so fast, and I tip precariously to the side. Oliver grabs my shoulder and stabilizes me before I fall to the ground. Again, his touch awakens a panic response. My breath turns shallow.

"Let's just try to make it to the library in one piece." Oliver laughs once more. "Who knows? Maybe I'll find something to read.... Maybe."

Our eyes meet before he lets go of my arm. For a moment, I can't tear my gaze away from his gray blue irises. There's some green peppered in random spots, reminding me of planet Earth as seen from space. Like an entire universe could be contained in a kid. I hurry onward, hoping he can't hear my heart drumming in my chest.

Glutton for punishment, Maybelline, Mama tuts in my ear.

"Whoa!" Oliver exclaims, oblivious. "This place is ancient!"

The library looms ahead of us, a guardian angel and the perfect distraction from the tug-of-war taking place in my brain. Half of me wants to trust Oliver and know him better, and the other half calls me stupid for ignoring Mama's most important advice. Every time I loosen up, she pops back into my head to knock some sense into me. Why can't I be careful and fun at the same time?

"I'm surprised it hasn't been condemned," Oliver comments, wobbling the front porch railing like a loose tooth. Shrugging, I breeze past him into the entryway, tossing my penny into the silver bucket so he can't see.

I wish critical Mama would leave me alone.

A weight lifts from my shoulders the instant I cross the threshold. The atmosphere of comfort hugs my worries away and I take a big deep breath while Oliver plugs his nose.

"Why does it smell like old people?" Oliver whispers behind his hand. Narrowing my eyebrows, I shoot him a glare and he pretends to zip his lips shut. Just label me a librarian-in-training. Mrs. Campbell hunches at the front desk, a corded phone held between her ear and shoulder while she types on her computer. She gives a crooked wave and almost drops the phone. I grab Oliver by his hoodie and pull him over to the normal-sized tables in the fiction section. Sharing my sanctuary is a bad idea.

Oliver rotates in his chair to absorb the space, and I snap my fingers at him, gesturing pointedly to his backpack. He withdraws a blank sheet of paper then casts a sheepish grin.

"Can I borrow a pencil... and your textbook?" he asks. I roll my eyes and pass over the necessary supplies. Oliver taps his pencil against the table in a rock-n-roll solo while I find the assignment page.

Little do I know, he's got a shorter attention span than Lucy hopped up on Halloween candy. Channeling his focus takes constant reminders... no easy task when somebody doesn't talk. I passed on ice cream for this? Part of me wants to march behind him and physically hold his head still so he can finish the few example problems.

Somehow, he reaches the finish line. While I'm checking, correcting, and explaining each missed step, Oliver manages to get ahold of my smiley face ball, lobbing it higher and higher into the air like a yellow missile. Next tutoring session I may bring some ropes to tie him still.

I'm only 50% joking... and 50% not.

His expression goes crestfallen when I show him the results—he's gotten three of the four problems wrong. Oliver slides the smiley ball over to me, puts up his hood, and crosses his arms. In-school Oliver returns.

"What's the point? Let's just call it," he mumbles, twisting his hoodie string tightly around his fingers. I push my chair right next to him with a loud sigh, angling my forefinger at his paper. Then I fix him with a hard stare and write a no nonsense note.

I'd like to see you try to leave.

"Math used to be my best subject, you know." Oliver scoops up the pencil and erases his incorrect answers so he can start from scratch.

What happened?

I scribe on an extra sheet of paper.

He looks at me hard, as if I've written in some foreign language. I pat his shoulder gently. Surprisingly, my anxiety doesn't flare when I touch him this time. Oliver leans away before answering.

"Life."

Well, everyone is good at something. You're braver than I am.

And I quickly sketch a skateboard to prove my point.

Oliver almost grins before throwing himself into a new set of equations. After a few minutes of frantic writing and erasing, he spins his paper around for me to see his work. I draw a star next to each correct answer. Four out of four. He can be taught.

"And you're a good teacher," Oliver says.

A warm, satisfied ripple cascades through my body, tingling along my spine.

It's not until I'm lying in bed that night and recounting the day's events, covers pulled to my chin in a plaid cocoon, that I realize during our study session I hadn't thought about checking my email.

Not once.

Chapter 19

BURNT TOAST ISN'T THE only thing stinking up the kitchen Tuesday morning. Though I've dressed for school, I'm still wiping the sleep from my eyes when feverish whispering collides with my drowsy brain. Uncle Mars tinkers with the toaster and I steer clear of the crispy hockey pucks stacked next to him. A granola bar and banana will do. Plunking into a chair, I relish my first gooey bite of banana. Once the brain fog clears, I tune into the hushed conversation between Lyla and Lucy at the table. Lyla angles close to Lucy, and Lucy whispers as only a kindergartener can—loud enough that the neighbors can hear every syllable.

"He had black curly hair and did a bunch of skateboard tricks..." Lucy giggles and sinks low in her seat when she notices me listening. Lyla's not one for beating around the bush.

"Maybelline, you made a new *friend*? Anyone I know?" Lyla picks at her fingernail, aloof, but I catch her glancing up to read my expression. Stay calm, Maybe. Lucy exaggerates all the time.

I shrug and chomp another bite of banana, but force myself to make eye contact with Lyla. She scowls and Lucy pops back into view.

"It's true, it's true! I saw a boy yesterday with Maybelline. They went to the library together." Lucy pouts as Lyla arches an eyebrow. "Why don't you believe me?"

"Maybelline was nice enough to help one of her classmates with his homework," Uncle Mars interjects. He's removed the underside of the toaster and fiddles with the wire connections. His voice sounds far away.

"Maybe doesn't talk to boys," Lyla says matter-of-factly.

"She could have talked to him telepally," Lucy shoots back.

"Telepathically, dear," Uncle Mars corrects and Lyla groans.

BAM. I pound a balled fist on the table that gets everyone's immediate attention. Uncle Mars even peels himself away from the toaster.

All eyes on me, I dramatically push back my chair, square my shoulders, and stomp out of the kitchen. The message translates, because the house stays quiet while I climb the stairs. Collecting my school things, the irritated heat lights me up and I swear steam may spew from my ears with the intensity of my outrage. But underneath my irritability lurks a deeper despair... am I changing that much? How will Mama respond when she comes back to get me?

Will she even recognize me?

****

Uncle Mars scrapes his car tire against the curb when he parks, even though he's wearing his cool guy sunglasses like an incognito secret agent. Immediately, I spot Oliver's curls huddled near the concrete steps with a group of random kids, all dressed in dark gray and black. They erupt in loud laughter as I exit the car. Oliver doesn't notice me, and I make a wide curve around the group to shoulder my way into the school, avoiding contact like I've never met him before. A heavy pit descends into my stomach. His other friends look way more fun than me.

"Morning, Maybelline!" Mrs. Nightingale chirps. I stand stiff in the doorway while she bustles through her office, opening the blinds and illuminating the dark corners. It would be nice if I could pull a string and let some brightness into my brain. I'm grumpy and I know it. Thankfully, Mrs. Nightingale doesn't seem to notice.

"How's the week been so far? I spoke with Miss Mendoza, and she was proud of your progress. Where's your stress level with school?" I display a solid seven fingers. "Progress is progress, no matter how small," Ms. Nightingale insists. She brandishes a colored sheet of paper and beckons me closer. I enter the room but don't sit down.

"Ms. Bennet scheduled the first newspaper meeting today, right after school. Here's the flier going around. I look forward to checking in with you and Oliver to see what you think. How exciting that Harper Lee will have its own paper!"

I take the sheet, skimming over it before stuffing it in my backpack. I point to the door, expressionless.

"Go on and have a spectacular day!" Mrs. Nightingale exclaims.

I can't remember ever having a day that was *actually* spectacular.

****

The bad mood restarts my brain loops, like the anxiety tornado can sense when I'm in a negative funk. By the end of the school day, I'm dizzy with worry. I'm sure if you listened close enough, you could hear the wind whistling in my overactive mind. Oliver waves when I meet him in class, but I think he picks up on my lack of enthusiasm because he's quieter than before. I don't ask him about the friends from earlier. He leaves me to my own devices, which is both a blessing and a curse. How can I explain my jumbled up feelings to someone else when I don't even understand them? But the lack of interaction makes me feel even worse.

The dismissal bell blares at the end of English, but Oliver and I stay seated at our desks while the rest of the kids slingshot out of the room. Oliver scribbles a note and passes it over to me.

Best Newspaper Names

Daily Doldrums

Doldrums means depressed or boring, I think. I almost laugh and tap my lips with my pen before adding my own creation:

The Shooting Star

We pass the list like a hot potato until a few other kids amble into the classroom, none of whom I recognize. Ms. Bennet flickers the lights and everyone shushes.

"History in the making," Ms. Bennet announces. "The birth of Harper Lee's school paper. Thank you for joining me on this endeavor! Your journalistic spirit inspires me!"

Ms. Bennet's voice gets high and pitchy, but I can tell she's being genuine by the sparkle in her eye. She really does love language. I retrieve my library journal from the depths of my bag and take an indulgent sniff. This is the first step on my journey to becoming a writer. Ms. Bennet's enthusiasm is catching 'cause cheerful butterflies flutter throughout my insides. It's a nice change, especially after this morning.

Turns out a newspaper has a ton of moving parts. The group lands on the name "Harper Lee Happenings;" pretty quickly but after that, every other decision becomes a debate. One of the students, Alan, provides the most objections. His cousin works for a big paper in New York City, which I guess translates to grade-A know-it-all status. Ms. Bennet's left eye twitches each time he makes a new comment.

"You should assign everyone a role for the paper, Ms. Bennet. That way the work stays organized," Alan comments. "Do you mind?" He doesn't wait for an answer, instead approaching the board and making a list of job titles and various columns. Next to the word supervisor, he writes his name. If I'm being honest, his printing isn't much better than chicken scratch.

Ms. Bennet massages her temples. "I do appreciate your input, Alan. It's important for the paper to be a team effort. As the teacher, I think I'll step into the supervisor role. But I'd be happy to give you the first choice for what column you'd like to represent."

"Well, my cousin always says the more dramatic the news, the better. I'd like to tackle a crime or mystery section." Alan straightens his wire-rimmed glasses and puffs out his chest.

Oliver snorts, breaking the stunned silence.

"Just because my Mom was a photographer doesn't make me a photo expert," Oliver whispers behind his hand to me. I blink at him curiously and he claps his hand over his mouth, as if he's spilled top secret information. An emotionless mask falls over his face, his eyes not meeting mine.

"Alan, much of the paper will focus on actual events at

our school. I'm not sure if a crime column would be applicable, but I'm happy to let you try. Maybe incorporate some safety tips as well." Ms. Bennet erases 'Supervisor' and writes 'Safety' next to Alan's name. "What would the rest of you like to work on?"

A curly-haired, doe-eyed girl named Tina claims the advice column, and another super tall girl, Lainey, chooses sports (she's got an in with the basketball team). Brett takes recent events, and artsy Claire volunteers for comics. The entire board transforms into an enormous list by the time Ms. Bennet gets to us. Oliver doodles on his hand. I nudge him sharply with my elbow.

"Since you'll be working as a pair, how about you and Maybelline take on the community connections column? You can write articles about the town of Salem." Ms. Bennet beams and Oliver shrugs. My back goes ramrod straight. I hope she can see how serious I am about this job. Ms. Bennet gives us a wink and jots our names in the only remaining blank space. The classroom air feels electrically charged. In-school Oliver returns and actually yawns. The nerve! I scribe a quick note to get his head in the game.

What should our first article be about?

"You can decide," Oliver mutters.

I'm going to need your help.

"I know."

Ms. Bennet flings open the classroom door, and students queue around her into the hall. Alan speaks under his breath to Claire, detailing how she should draw the newspaper comics. Claire brandishes a fist and he flusters, racing off down the hall.

"Be sure to have a proposal by next week. Then the real work begins!" Ms. Bennet exclaims.

Oliver and I fall into stride, our steps vibrating down the empty hallway. When we turn the corner and exit the building, the same group of darkly dressed kids from this morning waits at the bottom of the cement steps. One of the boys tries to ride his skateboard down the stair handrail with the noisy screech of metal on metal. He catches himself as he falls to the concrete. The front door closes with a bang and the group notices us at the top of the stairs. My heart rate accelerates.

"Hey, bud! How's it going? Did you have detention again?" A boy with blonde spikes and an earring in his left ear saunters up the steps and slaps Oliver on the back. Then the stranger looks at me, which makes me tingle all over, and not in a good way. My tongue feels glued to the roof of my mouth.

"Nah, not today," Oliver responds. "I'm actually working on some extra credit so my dad gets off my back."

"Who's your friend?" spikey boy inquires.

"Maybelline, meet Jack. Jack, this is my tutor Maybelline." Oliver keeps his eyes trained on the steps and I squirm from foot to foot, itching to run in the opposite direction. He called me his tutor. Not his friend.

"Parents are the worst. They should just mind their own business." Jack laughs. My stomach twists in knots. *Breathe*, says the quiet voice in the back of my head, but it's drowned out by uproarious laughter from the nearby kids. My stomach jolts like I might be sick. Panicking, I clench my jaw and bite my tongue to fight the nausea down.

"So what's your story?" Jack's staring at me again, with a glint in his eye not unlike those rowdy outlaws in Uncle Mars' favorite westerns. I shift on my feet and try to walk down the next staircase, flat out ignoring him. Jack grabs my backpack by the handle, holding me still.

"Do you speak English?" he asks. He's so close I can see the chip in his tooth and smell pizza on his breath.

Oliver steps between us.

"She's just shy. Besides, she's had a cold, so her voice is hoarse." Jack releases my backpack and gets nose to nose with Oliver. I take a few steps away, but something keeps me from running. I can't leave Oliver alone, not with the heavy cloud of looming confrontation.

"Charity friend? huh, Grant?" Jack jeers.

Oliver stiffens his shoulders but doesn't back down. "Maybelline's doing me a favor. I actually care about my future. You know, so my dad doesn't have to send me to military school."

Jack's facade cracks and his gaze flicks to his friends. "You said your dad wanted to send you to summer camp," one of the lankier boys pipes in. "Dude, military school... talk about extreme."

"I didn't ask your opinion," Jack seethes at the boy.

Oliver's upper lip twitches. Jack grabs ahold of the front of Oliver's hoodie with both hands. The rest of the kids jump to their feet, hooting like animals. I'm frozen where I stand.

"Why does everything have to be a drama fest, Jack? No harm, no foul, man. Just let us pass." Oliver grips Jack's fingers and slowly unbends them.

"You want to spend your time with a mute loser, be my guest," Jack says. He steps aside so Oliver can walk past. My chest relaxes the tiniest bit.

"Your mom's a mute loser," shouts an Asian kid with a choppy haircut.

"He doesn't have a mom," Jack whispers, so quiet I can barely hear him, but I know Oliver does by the way his face sinks, like all the joy and common sense has been ripped out of him. He meets my eyes for a split second and I know what he's going to do before he spins around. Using both hands, Oliver shoves Jack forcefully in the chest, sending him tumbling head over feet into the metal stair railing, with his left arm taking the brunt of the collision. The rest of the boys gasp and rush to help. From my vantage point, I can see Jack's arm bent at a peculiar angle, his face contorted with pain. The scene swims before me and I brace against the brick wall for support. Oliver doesn't even glance back. He stands rigid at the top of the stairs, facing away from the crowd, with his chest heaving and tears tracking down his cheeks.

Mr. Hill, the principal, comes running around the school, shouting for an ambulance into his phone. Oliver crumples to the ground, head quivering in his hands, collapsing like a marshmallow and craft stick building in the midst of an earthquake.

Chapter 20

UNCLE MARS APPEARS FROM the parking lot and joins the crowd as the ambulance approaches. Once Jack was on his way to the hospital with the paramedics, Uncle Mars accompanied me and Oliver to Mr. Hill's office, where we were invited to sit while Mr. Hill called Oliver's dad. My uncle studies the bookcases along the wall, and I fiddle with my smiley face ball, once in a while trying to catch Oliver's eye. He has flipped up his hood and slouches over in the chair, like he's pretending to be asleep. I know better by the twitch of his hoodie string as he wraps it tight around his finger. But I can't see underneath his hood.

Uncle Mars whistles as he thumbs through a thick hardcover, providing a tune for my brain's frantic dance. What will happen to Oliver? Will he be expelled? My breathing grows shallow as I contemplate losing my new friend—my only friend. The fight wasn't even his fault. Oliver's fury plays on the screen in my mind, and I remember experiencing a similar anger only once, a long time ago—before Mama left. I push the memory forcefully away as Mr. Hill and another tall man enter the office.

A pair of heavy leather work boots halt next to Oliver's chair. They belong to a kind-faced Black man wearing a tired frown. He's got thick, curly black hair, just like Oliver. His dark chestnut eyes betray his disappointment, but the wrinkles around his mouth suggest a history of smiling. I wonder if Oliver smiles when he's with his family, or if in-school Oliver follows him home.

Mr. Hill clears his throat. "Maybelline, you're free to go. Mrs. Nightingale will be in shortly to discuss Oliver's altercation."

I stand and take a step closer to Mr. Hill, my mouth opening of its own accord like the words are fighting to take action. *He's innocent! It was an accident! Punish me, too!* But speaking up means breaking my rules. Breaking my rules means jeopardizing my chances of reconnecting with Mama, and nothing good comes from being bold. My darkest memory threatens to surface, so my mouth clunks shut, and I swallow my protests whole. Uncle Mars takes my hand and leads me away. Still Oliver won't look up. His dad gives us a gentle nod as we pass, and the office door closes behind us with a foreboding thud. Those unspoken words sour in my mouth, tasting of failure and regret, like a blackened piece of toast, bitter and gross.

****

"Oliver won't be in school today. Harper Lee has a zero-tolerance policy for violence," Mrs. Nightingale fills me in the next morning. Dark circles accent her droopy eyelids, and she hasn't even poured herself a cup of tea. I wonder if I look the same, teetering in the middle of the room with my shoes planted firmly on the carpet so I don't topple over from my frayed nerves.

"He'll be back at school on Monday. If you like, I can assign a new class partner for you, so you'll feel more comfortable. I know the exchange must have brought up some... traumatic memories." Mrs. Nightingale rubs her forehead.

My pulse quickens and I emphatically shake my head no. No, no, no... I can't explain it, but the prospect of school without Oliver feels way more overwhelming than our current arrangement. This strange realization punches me in the gut.

Mrs. Nightingale raises an eyebrow. "Well, if that's the case, I could use your help with something," she continues. "Will you take notes and collect assignments for Oliver? I can have his dad pick up the homework material on Friday afternoon."

The memory of Oliver stepping between me and Jack grants me extra courage. A lightbulb flips on in my brain and

I bite at the inside of my cheek. Lately, I'm just full of surpris-es—even for myself. Scooping a pencil from Mrs. Nightin-gale's desk, I write a note on one of her colorful post-its.

I can give him the assignments if you want. I'd just need his address.

Her eyes go wide and she takes a couple extra blinks. Nope, she's not hallucinating. Maybelline Reed has officially left the building. Since when do I volunteer for one-on-one time with a boy? Mrs. Nightingale copies his address on my post-it before I head to my first class, my pulse SOS-ing on my wrist.

Mama's voice haunts me for the rest of the school day. *Don't say I didn't warn you.*

****

Oliver lives within a mile of our house. 23 Oak Court, Salem, Illinois. Just a few blocks away from my beloved li-brary. Something about this realization feels heavy and hopeful, at the same time.

Uncle Mars loops the car a few times around the cul-de-sac before deciding to pull into Oliver's driveway (loops are everywhere when you're looking). The two-story house stands quiet and lifeless, almost like a model home. I gulp as I unbuckle my seat belt, begging the air to cooperate with my tightening lungs. Seeing Oliver at home is no different than seeing him at school or the library. Strictly business, plain and simple.

Why, oh why can't I breathe?

"Take your time, honey," Uncle Mars says as he flips on the radio. The loud thwack of my car door sends a flock of nearby birds whizzing through the sky. I bite my pinky fin-gernail as I mount the steps and, trembling, press the door-bell. My loops twist tighter and tighter the longer I wait on the porch.

Finally, after what feels like an eternity, the door cracks open. I stumble backwards when I register the new face. The figure has the same cheekbones as Oliver but short black hair and lankier overall height. He hurries on to the porch as if to catch me when I stumble.

"Whoa there, everything alright?" the boy asks. In the

sunlight, I recognize more subtle similarities. Same warm skin tone and friendly gray eyes, but definitely older than Oliver. The teenager scratches the back of his neck. I step further away, willing my heartbeat to slow.

"Are you lost?" he questions, peering toward the driveway. Upon noticing Uncle Mars, the boy raises a slightly confused hand in welcome and pokes his head back into the house. "Oliver, I think you've got company."

Oliver appears in the doorway and blinks a few times. I half-wave at him. "Hey, Maybelline," he mumbles.

"Aiden, we're gonna head over to the playground for a bit," Oliver continues, leaning against the screen door.

"Sorry, bro. Dad grounded you. No off-campus trips." Aiden gives a raspy laugh. "But feel free to hang on the porch if you want to be outside."

Oliver scowls as Aiden pats his shoulder and waves good-bye to both of us. A car pulls into the cul-de-sac and he piles in among the teenagers before it chugs out of view. Oliver sighs and sits on the porch swing, rocking it back and forth with his toe.

"That doofus is my brother, though you probably figured it out," Oliver confirms. I prop myself against the porch post versus settling in next to him on the swing. The fluttery butterflies have returned to my stomach. *Strictly business,* I remind them. *Nothing to see here.*

"What's up?" Oliver asks, watching me intently. A frog croaks somewhere in answer, and I point to my backpack with enthusiasm. When he notices the extra textbooks, his expression softens like melting ice cream.

"At least now I don't have to play catch up. I don't need to give Dad another reason to ground me," Oliver admits. "Thanks, Maybelline. I owe you."

I shake my head and heat floods to my cheeks. Then I touch my chest before patting his shoulder, hoping he understands my gratitude. He didn't have to step between me and Jack, but he did. Emboldened by his amused grin, I scribble a note on a piece of looseleaf.

Friends help friends.

Could be glare from the sun, but I swear Oliver's cheeks take on a deeper hue. The butterflies flap into a frenzy and my mouth goes dry. Neither one of us looks each other in the eye for a long awkward minute. The noisy frog croaks again. I peek over the porch railing, on the hunt for slimy green skin hidden amongst the hydrangeas.

"Do you have time to hang out for a little bit? We could talk about the newspaper article if you want. My dad should be home soon, and I'm bored by myself. Aiden doesn't spend a lot of time at home." Oliver's face falls a bit, like he's tripped on a memory, and I hold up an index finger. I rush back to the car. Loud music blasts from inside, and I knock on the window to break Uncle Mars out of concert mode. He stops mid head bang and rolls down the glass.

"What's up, kiddo?"

I gesture toward Oliver's house and hold up my backpack, hands stitched together in a plea. Uncle Mars checks his phone before giving me a thumbs up.

"I can run a few errands and be back in an hour. How does that sound?" Nodding, I step backward so he can pull out of the driveway and urge the loops in my head to behave. *Breathe, Maybelline, breathe.* Now's my chance to kickstart my career as a writer and possibly learn a little more about Oliver in the process.

How do I swat away a stomach full of butterflies?

Chapter 21

OLIVER HOLDS THE SCREEN door open with his foot, and I tiptoe past him. When we're shut inside, my heart rate skyrockets, blood whooshing in my ears. The hairs on the back of my neck are on end, screaming a warning, "Mistake!" But my butterflies seem tickly instead of panicked. Can anything good feel like anxiety?

"So, this is the living room. We can work here," Oliver mumbles. He flips on a couple of lights while I drift around the room, absorbing the woodwork and comfortable furnishings. A rustic stone fireplace punctuates the space, and I'm drawn toward it.

"Be right back. Gotta get my tablet," he says before leaping up the stairs. A series of picture frames atop the wooden mantle have hooked my interest. Most of the collection hosts school pictures of Oliver and Aiden fake smiling in front of different photo backdrops while wearing button-up shirts and mini bow-ties. As the brothers get older, smiles shift to rebellious poker faces. There's a more recent photo of the two boys posing with their dad in front of a Christmas tree. Aiden is elbowing Oliver, and Oliver is laughing, instead of scowling.

On the end of the mantle stands the tiniest frame. I have to hold it close to my face to see the details of the scene. A pretty tanned lady lounges on the beach with a toddler in her lap. Upon closer inspection, I recognize Oliver by his dimples and curly dark hair. He's got a pair of women's sunglasses slung across his face, and the lady's head tilts back in exuberant laughter. Pure happiness captured in a photo. I can imagine the summer heat against my skin and the grit of sand between my toes for the briefest moment.

The thud of footsteps coming down the stairs interrupts my snooping, and I shove the picture back on the mantle before hunkering down on an armchair. The picture piques my interest, but I don't know how to ask him about it.

"We could research places in Salem we might want to write about," Oliver plops on the couch and rests his feet atop the coffee table while he scrolls on his tablet. My heartrate evens out, and I retrieve my library journal and pen, uncapping it so I'm prepared. Oliver glaces at me and grins.

"I dub you Maybe the official note-taker," he laughs and waves me closer. A glob of spit gathers in my throat, but I move to sit next to him on the couch. Together, we collect a list of what we deem article-worthy locations: Mario's Pizza, Town Hall, Salem Aquarium, and Silver Flix Movie Theater make the initial cut. My stomach grumbles at the mention of the movie theater, and Oliver calls a time-out to pop us some popcorn. Salt and butter explode in my mouth on the first bite. We take turns tossing kernels into the air and trying to catch them on our tongues. Finally, winded from laughter, we return to note-taking. Our hour's almost up.

We should come up with some theme questions for the article. Once we've brainstormed, we can pick the best ones for the interviews.

My cursive loops and twirls, more careless than I've ever written before. But I crunch another mouthful of popcorn and order my anxiety to stuff it.

We probably should have asked know-it-all Alan which questions to use.

Oliver nearly spits out his sip of water when he reads that comment, and I grin from ear to ear, only slightly worried I've got kernels stuck in my teeth.

"You're funny, Maybelline. I'm glad we're on the same team." Oliver shuts down his tablet and a car horn honks outside. Uncle Mars, back already. That was the fastest hour of my life. True to form, my brain loops around in constant whirls, but the repetitive thoughts are not entirely unpleasant. Mostly, I'm replaying the fun we've had and the potential for our newspaper article. With Oliver's help, we could be famous in our little town. He'll speak and I'll write.—the perfect combo for success.

A key jangles in the latch as we approach the front door, and when it swings open, Oliver's dad appears on the threshold. He thumps his heavy work boots on the step to knock off extra dirt, and my breath catches, hoping he won't be mad that I've visited without his knowledge. Oliver beats him to the punch.

"Dad, this is my friend Maybelline. She brought my homework over and we've been studying together." Oliver itches the back of his head and averts his gaze. My heart soars clear up to the ceiling and I'm flooded with happiness. He finally called me his friend.

"Great to officially meet you, Maybelline." Oliver's dad looms above us in the entryway, but his voice is gentle. He shakes my hand and gives me a little nod. "Thank you for dropping his schoolwork. Oliver's grounded, so we'll save more study sessions for next week or after."

"Okay, Dad. She was just leaving." Oliver hooks my backpack in a steel grip and pulls me onto the porch, shutting the door with a thud behind him. I wiggle my eyebrows so he'll crack a smile.

"He's always gotta have the last word," Oliver mumbles. He still hasn't let go of my backpack. My heart pounds, but I don't pull away. Adrenaline courses through my body like electricity. "I'll see you on Monday, then?"

Skipping to the car, I hold up my library journal so he gets the message.

"Don't worry, I won't forget," Oliver promises.

And I believe him. Sort of.

Chapter 22

WHEN WE GET HOME, Aunt Julie greets us at the front door, her shoulders stiff as she plays with the hem of her shirt. She and Uncle Mars share a meaningful look, and he veers up the stairs to check on Lucy and Lyla. Leaving me and Aunt Julie in the entryway—alone. My mood sinks faster than a penny in the wishing bucket, and the popcorn threatens to make a comeback.

"Maybelline, dear. While you were out, your Mama called," Aunt Julie whispers, wringing her hands. The news hits me square in the jaw like an uppercut, and I sway like I may faint. Luckily, the wall catches my elbow and Aunt Julie grabs the other. I haven't spoken directly to Mama in *years*. Why now? And how did I miss it? My light-hearted joy dissolves as my stomach acid churns. To make matters worse, I've also caught the hiccups. Whoopee.

"Hic."

Aunt Julie guides me to the nearby padded bench and helps me sit.

"Hic."

I watch her expectantly, though my hands grip my thighs so tight that I'm sure there will be fingerprint bruises as evidence.

"Hic."

Why won't she speak up already?

"Hic."

Finally... "Your Mama asked about your schooling. She said you'd emailed her about starting middle school. She gives you her love but doesn't know when she'll be able to visit." Aunt Julie bites on her bottom lip as she breaks the news.

"Hic."

She's not coming to see me? To get me? To bring me home?

"Hic."

And if she saw my email, why didn't she email me back? Why didn't she *ever* email me back? None of it makes sense. Tears sting underneath my eyelids as a nasty sliver of disappointment stabs through my chest. Mama's fine without me. She's never needed me like I need her.

The hiccups stop, snuffed out by my fear.

"Maybelline, your Mama called solely to ask about you. I'm sure she'll call back and catch up soon." Aunt Julie won't meet my eyes.

I don't want to stick around to debate with her. I climb the stairs in a daze and slam my bedroom door, chest heaving. Muted voices from downstairs drift underneath the door. Aunt Julie telling Uncle Mars about Mama. Red hot rage powers through me and I grab one of the pillows on my bed, press it to my face, and scream at the top of my lungs. Every inch of me burns as if I'm on fire from the inside out.

Screaming isn't the same as talking. Ask anybody.

****

Walk Two Moons comes to the rescue. After my mini-meltdown, I hole up in my room until bedtime, curled under my blanket with the musty book propped on my knees. Aunt Julie brings me a grilled cheese sandwich and I nibble the toasted bread while I get to know Salamanca Tree Hiddle. She's different from me, but not *so* different from me. Her mother left too, except Salamanca takes a road trip with her grandparents to find her. My grandparents live in a nursing home all the way in Michigan. I could take a road trip to see them, but they won't be driving to me any time soon. Besides, I don't know where to start looking for Mama, so we'd only drive in circles. More endless loops. Still, Salamanca reaches through the pages and squeezes me around the shoulders because she understands.

School on Thursday and Friday passes by in a blur. The

empty seat next to me drags my attention from most of the lessons. Is Oliver working on our article? Does he like being by himself, or is he lonely? At-home Oliver smiles more than in-school Oliver... but that picture I found replays in my brain as proof that toddler-Oliver was happiest of all.

Much to my surprise, Aunt Julie shows up to get me from school. She interprets my blinked-morse-code-question as I open the car door.

"How about you and I have some fun time together before therapy," Aunt Julie says, studying me in the rearview mirror. She has the same eyes as Mama, I realize with an inward gasp. How haven't I noticed before? Except Mama was fearless and carefree, while Aunt Julie's eyes scrunch at the edges like she's trying to solve a difficult math problem. Maybelline plus anxiety multiplied by Oliver and divided by therapy equals...what? Guilt bites at my heart the same way I chew on my fingernails. Aunt Julie's not responsible for fixing me, but she thinks she should.

Aunt Julie pulls into the parking lot for the local coffee shop, Salem Sips, a comfy corner storefront with iron coffee cups hung by the door as lanterns. My aunt knows the menu forward and backward... Uncle Mars calls her a coffee connoisseur. Aunt Julie says it's her guilty pleasure, because every dental professional knows coffee stains your teeth. The promise of coffee always puts some pep in her step, and I jog after her into the shop.

Waves of espresso, chocolate, and crumbly cookie smells massage my nose, and I tap my toe to the catchy jazz playlist while we wait in line. Salem Sips opened a few years ago and Aunt Julie has single-handedly made them a hit. Just kidding of course, but the owner once joked they're going to name a drink after her because of all her customer referrals. You'd think Aunt Julie had won the lottery by the way her eyes twinkled.

"One mocha latte and a hot chocolate, please." Aunt Julie snaps open her pocketbook and hands over a worn rewards card while I wander the store admiring the colorful mugs and keychains for sale. *Brew can do it, Espresso yourself,* and *Where you bean all my life.* Cheesy, but creative. I make mental notes to remember puns as an option for our article.

"Order up!" the barista exclaims. Aunt Julie hands me

my cardboard cup and leads me to a pair of plush chairs next to the faux fireplace. I lift the steaming hot cocoa under my nose and take an exaggerated whiff of rich chocolate with hints of whipped cream and sweet caramel. My mouth waters, but I hold back, giving the treat time to cool.

"Are you feeling better about public school, Maybe?" Aunt Julie crosses her legs, sips her coffee slowly, and releases a delicate sigh. Coffee contentment. Her favorite hobby.

I shrug and sip my hot chocolate, letting the drips settle and dissolve on my tongue in a rush of sugary goodness.

"How about Oliver? Does it help to have a friend in class?" Aunt Julie sets down her coffee on a nearby end table. Uh-oh. This talk just turned serious. *Play it cool, Maybelline.*

Shrugging again, I arch my gaze around the coffee shop, absorbing the customers relaxing in all the nooks and crannies. A tingle down my spine alerts me to Aunt Julie's close attention. My eyes catch on a young woman in the corner, clicking away on a laptop, fingertips a blur of inspiration. A real life writer! Oliver and I should work on our article at Salem Sips.

Aunt Julie clears her throat. "Sweetheart, you know I'm here for you, right?" she whispers.

Ripping my attention away from my writing fantasies, I nod, but a dense pit forms in my stomach. Aunt Julie only wants to have "fun time" because she feels sorry for me. The incline of her eyebrows and twitch of her lips betray the ulterior motive. Pity party for two. The missed phone call memory bursts back into existence, plowing through any good feelings. I need to get out of this closed-in space. I need air!

Mama strikes again.

Sniffling the snot back into my nose, I point to the door. Aunt Julie's face sags, but she gathers her drink and purse. Lost to silent worries, we exit the coffee shop together but somehow universes apart.

Chapter 23

THE OPPRESSIVE SILENCE WEIGHS on us the whole way to the therapist's office. Aunt Julie hugs me before finding a seat in the lobby, and I knock on Miss Mendoza's open office door. She swivels in her chair and waves me inside, her beautiful jade green blouse an exact complement to her eyes.

"Let's start with breathing," she instructs, flipping on the meditative music as I sink onto the couch. Tight bands twist around my lungs, and I cross my fingers as the exercise begins. *Please calm me down.* Hints of flowery lavender tickle my senses from the purple candle flickering in the corner.

"Picture your lungs as a balloon. Imagine the balloon inflating when you hear the initial chime and deflating with the second chime." Miss Mendoza's gentle instructions siphon some of the tension from my chest and shoulders. I envision a yellow smiley face balloon growing and deflating with each of my breaths. The clock ticks, rhythmic, as the ebb and flow of fresh air grounds me.

When the music stops, I blink open my eyes and wipe away a few sneaky tears. The precious stress relief gives me hope again. Miss Mendoza must be magic to quiet Mama's voice the way she does.

"Well done, Maybelline. Excellent focus." She smiles, writing some notes in my folder. Reaching over to her desk, she retrieves a white board and marker and hands the supplies to me. "On a scale of one (not so great) to ten (awesome), how was your week?"

Fingers trembling, I write *4*. Miss Mendoza will know if

I'm fibbing. But how come honesty is so scary? I'm floundering through a fishbowl while the whole world is watching.

She nods and writes more notes, her face passive and calm.

The exact opposite of me.

"Can you think of any reasons this week may have challenged you?" Miss Mendoza gestures to the white board. I try to click my marker. It doesn't work.

Oliver got in trouble.

"I can see how that would be upsetting, especially since you've made such a good team. Did anything else bother you at school?"

No.

"How about at home?"

Pausing, I bite the marker cap. Moment of truth. Should I say it?

She'll find out anyway.

Mama called.

Miss Mendoza stares at me but says nothing. I hang my head so my hair falls across my face like a curtain. The golden waves remind me of Mama, except she always kept her hair tied back. After all, neatness matters.

"Tell you what. Let's get creative." Miss Mendoza collects the white board and pulls out some paper and colored pencils from her closet. "I know it's tough to think about your Mama, and she's been on your mind a lot lately. Can you draw me some memories you have of her? We'll start with one good memory and one not-so-good memory. Are you up for that?"

If only Oliver were here; he's way better at art than me. But he also doesn't know my Mama.

I guess it's worth a shot to get rid of some of the ickiness inside. When I open the box of colored pencils, Miss Mendoza shares a radiant smile.

"I'll leave you to it," she says. She stands up and actually exits the room, shutting the door with a small click.

Courage surges from my brain to my toes once I'm alone. I can do this. I'll conjure a good memory first.

Our apartment in springtime. Mama opened the windows and the aroma of flowers floated through every cranny. She sat at the kitchen table with a checkbook balanced on her knee, leafing through envelopes of mail. Mama always got quiet when sorting the mail. Usually her personality coated the apartment like a bold paint, commanding attention. On mail days, I'd grab a stack of picture books from my room and stretch out on the carpet, soaking in the silence and my imagination. Warm sunshine on my back made me sleepy, but I'd fight to stay awake for my stories.

That day I got curious and wandered, barefoot, into the kitchen. The cool tile tickled my toes. Mama had a pen pressed to a check, swirling and twirling the ballpoint like a ballerina dancer. I'd learned the alphabet in school, but Mama's alphabet was fancy, tied together as strands of ink ribbon. She noticed me watching and plucked me off the floor, into her lap.

"What are you doing, Mama?" I asked with a yawn. She stroked my hair, sending tingles along my spine.

"Boring grown-up stuff, baby," Mama yanked the check clear of the others with a rip and set it on top of an envelope.

With the tip of my finger, I traced along her writing real slow, trying to find recognizable letters in the beautiful curves.

Mama hugged me tight and whispered in my ear. "Would you like to learn cursive, Maybelline?"

My brain got all dizzy and my eyes crossed with how fast I nodded. Mama giggled, swiping the boring papers off the table with a swish of her arm. She showed me how cursive letters connect to one another to form one cohesive word. Just like me and Mama sitting linked at the kitchen table. On that lovely afternoon, she taught me to spell my name in shaky cursive... how to make my pen dance like it was on a stage. And every day since, I've practiced, so I can show Mama my incredible letter ballet when she comes back to get me.

My picture has bright colors and confident strokes... me in Mama's lap, both of us giggling. Mama's lilting voice echoes with the memory, as if she may be standing just out of sight. Sighing, I set the drawing to the side and take a blank sheet of paper. There are lots of bad memories to choose from, two conflicting versions of Mama yet both equally real. I pinpoint an especially clear moment. The beginning of the end: my introduction to the angry man.

Tap, tap, tap. The knock on the door interrupted Ms. Tina's soaps. Her chair squeaked as she stood and rustled to the doorway. I collected my books and pranced after her. Ms Tina unlatched the lock, and muffled conversation reverberated underneath the door, through the small gap...two voices. Mama wasn't alone. A thick wad of saliva settled in the back of my throat. She rarely brought any "friends" home to our apartment. An uneasy heaviness pushed against my shoulders, squashing my mood.

Sure enough, a big man stood behind Mama, his frame nearly as broad as Ms. Tina's entire apartment door. Scooting up against Mama's skirt, I grabbed her hand and dropped my eyes, hoping the man would just keep talking. Possibly even say goodnight and leave.

"Maybelline, pumpkin, don't be shy," Mama stepped to the side. A whoosh of cold air engulfed me, and I tossed my head back, teeth chattering, to greet the man. His mouth smiled, but his eyes burned. I never remembered his name.

"She's not normally this reserved." Mama laughed, bopping a painted fingernail on the tip of my nose. "Shake his hand, honey. Be polite."

My quivering hand extended and the man's enormous palm swallowed it up, nerves prickling up my arm at his touch. The angry man squeezed like he was crushing a mosquito. I winced, but Mama had already moved on to unlock our apartment.

"Why don't you go play in your room, baby?" Mama stroked my bangs and pinched my cheek. I made sure to close my bedroom door all the way and lock the handset. Only then did my heart stop crashing in my ears.

Mama always said boys were no good. So why would she bring a boy with burning eyes into our home? Some questions go unanswered.

Side by side, my pictures contrast like vanilla to chocolate. The memory with the angry man shaking my hand is crafted of shadows; dark details etched on both the paper and my brain. No doubt Miss Mendoza will find a lot to unpack in these drawings. In truth, I'd rather take a long nap. Every muscle in my body sags and I release an enormous yawn. Leaning back on the sofa, I steal a minute of peace, covering both eyes to pretend I'm lounging in Salem Public

Library while Mrs. Campbell tip-taps away on her keyboard.

Mrs. Campbell may be a librarian, but I'm absolutely positive she'd never let an angry man with burning eyes into the library.

And neither would I.

Chapter 24

"YOU CAN DO BETTER than that," Alan's annoying voice whines like nails on a chalkboard. At our weekly Tuesday meeting, the Harper Lee Happenings crew have pushed the desks into a circle to share proposals, and Oliver half-heartedly reads our interview questions aloud. Alan cut him off after the first two questions.

"My cousin says meaningful questions lead to meaningful answers. We have to ask questions that no one has ever asked before." Alan stands on his chair, thrusting his pen toward the ceiling in a battle charge. "No risk, no reward!"

Ms. Bennet covers her face with her palm, muffling her response. "Alan, please take a seat. As chief safety journalist, your title requires wise choices." Ms. Bennet levels her gaze straight at him, pointing a rigid finger at his chair. "Namely, no climbing on furniture."

With a heavy sigh, Alan dismounts his soap box and resumes scribbling in his notebook.

"Now, then. Oliver, why don't you continue?" Ms. Bennet takes a deep breath, and a teensy twitch pulses in her right eye, as if she's about to lose her last nerve. I can't blame her. Alan is a preschooler in a sixth grader's body.

"Sure." Oliver runs a pencil along the questions as he reads. "What's the best part of working in Salem? How long have you been open? What's one thing you want the world to know about Salem, Illinois? Do you have any upcoming events you'd like to share with our readers?"

Ms. Bennet nods with each progressive question; her

eye twitching has also stopped. "Those are a great start, kids. Be sure you pick a common theme for your questions so you can blend them into one article. But I think you've got a solid foundation here."

Oliver high fives me under the desk. Or would that be a low five? Another step closer to official authorhood. My heart flies up, up, up like a helium balloon. Who knew that elevated heart rate could actually feel good!

"Now. You all have appropriate questions for the newspaper. We'll need to draft our articles next week to have them ready for release by the end of the month. Please conduct your interviews by then. I'm proud of your work so far!" Ms. Bennet opens the classroom door with a wide grin, eyes flicking to Alan as she tells us farewell. We push our desks back to their original spots and filter out of the classroom.

"Are you ready for the interviews?" Oliver asks.

Walking shoulder to shoulder through the tiled hall, our steps echo in satisfying synchronicity. Warmth bubbles in my stomach. 'We' feels natural now.

I give him a thumbs up and mimic Alan's victorious stance, arm thrust above me. Oliver snorts, then doubles over in fits of laughter.

"We... can do an interview... each day after school... to spread them out." Oliver gasps, clutching his ribcage.

Somehow, I'm not bothered at the idea of spending more time with him. Having a friend, even a boy, is actually fun. *Just hope he doesn't get tired of you,* Mama says in the back of my brain. I take a quick sniff of my library journal and the worry goes away. Oliver has nothing in common with the angry man. Halting in my tracks, shock vibrates through my core. My eyes slip shut as a new possibility rises to the surface of my thoughts. Mama... could be wrong. And if she was wrong about this, what else could she be wrong about?

"Hey, are you okay?" Oliver places a hand on my shoulder, and I shake my head to clear it. His touch wakes my butterflies and they flutter against my skin, making a trail of goosebumps. Oliver's planetary irises swirl with concern. I grin, stick out my tongue and race down the hall, shoes slapping loudly against the tile. Oliver's footfalls follow mine and we burst from the school into the sunlight, chests heaving, skin glowing with energy. Uncle Mars waves to me from the pick-up line. Oliver gives me a fist bump before we head our separate ways then sticks his tongue out as we drive past him on the street. I can't help but smile.

"Oh, Maybe, I bought you a newspaper while I was out today. Thought you could use it for inspiration on your article!" Uncle Mars tosses a plastic-wrapped bundle into the backseat. The big black letters across the top read "SALEM TIMES." Blowing him a kiss, I rip through the plastic and fan the newspaper across my lap. A real newspaper could make the difference to the authenticity of our article. I pour over the pages, thrilling in the smell of fresh ink. Books have more subtle scents, but newspapers are pungent. Ink and paper hot off the printer. As I flip through the pages, excitement pulses through me like the whirring of machines in a busy print room.

My attention latches onto one of the articles closest to the end. I catch my breath as the bold black title screams in my face. The words on the page roar and shatter the fragile hope residing in my heart. I read it again, and again, and again, certain I've misunderstood, until Uncle Mars pries the paper from my hands and holds me by the shoulders while tears wash my happy feelings far, far away.

SALEM LIBRARY SET TO CLOSE

My chest goes hollow, like someone has ripped it open. Where can I possibly go from here? How do I survive without my heart?

****

Dragging the curtains closed in my room to block out the sunlight, I rip off my shoes and climb into bed, fully clothed, my legs and arms numb, but my eyes on fire. The crying won't stop. A steady flow of tears and snot gunk up my blanket, and I burrow deeper under the covers, wishing I could turn back the clock to our newspaper meeting this afternoon. To be happy and unaware that everything was about to fall apart. The library...*my* library will be wiped off the map. My hands ball into fists and suddenly I'm choking on my thick sadness, drowning in the complete and utter despair of losing my safe place. Tossing the covers off, I tuck my knees below my chin and take ragged gasps of breath. *Please,*

please don't let them take the library away.

A gentle knock against the door signals me to twist the opposite direction, so it looks like I'm sleeping. I tense every shaking muscle, forcing myself perfectly still. A sliver of light appears across my bedroom wall, and little footsteps pad toward the bed.

"Maybelline," Lucy whispers.

I scrunch my eyes shut until they hurt. Lucy grows so quiet that I almost think she left. A light pressure descends on the bed behind me. Nope. Her hip presses into my back.

"My teacher says that crying is how our feelings get all squeaky clean, so we're ready to feel good again," Lucy fidgets and places what feels like a pillow against my shoulder.

I do my best not to jerk away, concentrating instead on even breaths.

She leans close to my ear and whispers again, "I'm glad you live with us, Maybe." She plants a kiss against my hair and disappears out into the hallway.

Once I'm positive she's gone, I spin around to toss away her pillow. Except the parting gift is not a pillow. It's Grover—her favorite plush unicorn, the one with the rainbow mane and hooves. She got him for her birthday last year and has cuddled with him every bedtime since.

Grover stares expectantly at me with his goofy grin and I can't help but choke a laugh. Am I as pitiful as a kindergartener now? But I scoop Grover up and hold him tight to my chest, brushing his sparkly mane against my face. He smells of lollipops and Lucy dreams. He works his magic and my tears run dry.

Cousins might not be so bad after all.

Chapter 25

WHEN TOMORROW COMES, I'VE fallen into a muted state of nothingness. No emotions, no energy, no optimism. Overnight, sleep kept its distance, and my normal morning routine requires tenfold effort. Aunt Julie doesn't rush me, but I don't get downstairs until everyone else has already packed into the car. She hands me a granola bar with an empathetic smile. I accept the granola bar; but put it in my backpack. Who knows if my stomach can handle food right now? The last thing I want is to throw up.

Lyla sits in the front passenger seat and Lucy's in the back with me. I'm met with complete silence in the car, so clearly Aunt Julie issued strict directions not to bother me. An entire SUV of Maybellines. The universal quiet makes my skin crawl. Lucy's head is pressed against her window and her little legs jiggle against the seat like she may explode. Poor kid. Every now and again she glances over at me, lips pinched together. The ride to school takes practically an eternity, especially since we have to drop Lucy at the elementary school first. We're so late that I don't even have time to check in with Mrs. Nightingale. Instead, I sleepwalk to first period.

Oliver's eyes get big when I enter the class with the final bell, and my stomach instantly drops. He's going to ask me what's wrong. The last time I pushed him away he got really upset, but I don't have the energy to explain the hopelessness inside me. I hope this time he understands.

Oliver reaches in his backpack and my heart rate slows. He's not going to quiz me right away, thank goodness. But wait, what's this? He sets an object on my desk right next to my trembling hand, then pulls back for the big reveal. A shiny new blue pen. A shiny new blue *clicky* pen. My mouth falls open. I don't remember telling him about my love for clicky pens. Inscribed along the side of the pen are tiny words: *"Write what should not be forgotten."* I press my thumb against the end for that soothing *click*. A trickle of calm seeps through the numbness.

Thank you, I mouth, and Oliver winks. We exist in companionable silence the rest of the school day, but my new pen doesn't leave my hand. It helps to know I'm not alone, especially with a ginormous library-shaped black hole looming behind me.

Once we're outside after school, Oliver finally pries.

"How has everything been, Maybe?" His forehead creases and I turn my attention to a ladybug crawling along a jagged crack in the sidewalk to avoid making eye contact. Shrugging, I stuff my hands in my pockets and wish Uncle Mars would appear, but his red jeep is only a tiny dot at the end of the pick-up line. Every second that passes, my loops twist faster.

"Do you want to work on an interview today? We could visit Town Hall. It's only a few blocks from my house." When I don't answer, Oliver slips straight into my line of view, bending down so we're nose to nose. My chest tightens like a taut rubber band. He's not going to drop it.

The red Jeep inches closer and I consider jogging down the row of cars to escape. My gaze darts between Oliver and my ride like a ping-pong ball. He must sense my thoughts because Oliver takes a step back to give me some breathing room.

"What about going to the library?" he asks. "I could use more help with math."

The painful cracks in my heart deepen and stretch until I'm sure I'll fall apart right there in front of Harper Lee Middle School. The endless line of cars blurs together and my sense of direction goes kaput. My loops spin so quickly that the world spins with them like an out-of-control top. Clutching my hands over my ears, I tip sideways and sink to the earth, landing hard on my bottom with a smack. My library journal tumbles out of my hands. Pain shoots up my spine, but nothing can compare to the horrible heartache radiating through each and every one of my cells. Oliver jumps into action, crouching low on the sidewalk to hover over me as a fresh supply of tears spills down my cheeks.

"Maybelline, I'm sorry. I don't know what I did," Oliver whispers and extends his arms as if to hug me but freezes partway. I crumple into his chest because the tears won't stop, and students drift past on either side of us, staring like I'm some kind of museum exhibit. Shame burns hot inside me at these stupid uncontrollable emotions. Oliver wraps his arm around my shoulders and, with my ear to his chest, I breathe to the rhythm of his heartbeat. *In and out, in and out.* Right up until the slam of a car door and hurried footsteps come closer. Uncle Mars.

"What's going on?" Uncle Mars stoops low, crooking a finger under my chin so I have to look at him. My nose blows an extra large snot bubble as I exhale and I pull up my shirt collar, covering the bottom half of my face, humiliated.

"I asked if she wanted to study at the library," Oliver replies, trembling as he hands my journal back to me.

"I see," Uncle Mars pats Oliver on the back and lifts me to my feet. A bunch of kids have gathered around us and whisper to each other behind their hands. Cheeks hot, I beeline for the car. Oliver lingers on the sidewalk. A conflict tugs at his face, but then he opens the back passenger door.

"Do you mind if I ride with you? Maybelline and I could hang at the playground." Oliver's expression hardens. "I want to make sure she's all right."

My stomach drops. The playground. Across the street from the library. Tears drip-drop off my nose. How much sadness can live inside a person? Too much.

"What do you say, kiddo?" Uncle Mars asks. Oliver can't change the situation with the library, but at least I won't be alone with these terrible thoughts.

A miniscule nod and Oliver slides into the backseat, buckling his seatbelt at once. He's gone tense and squeezes his backpack where it rests on his lap, his grip tight. Is he... nervous? Narrowing my eyes, I watch him closely on the drive to the playground. By the time we arrive, a dozen droplets of sweat decorate his forehead. He's shut his eyes as if he's praying... or asleep. But, when Uncle Mars parks the car, Oliver immediately whips open his door and bounds out. We're left in a dazed silence.

"Are you sure you'll be all right?" Uncle Mars reaches back a hand and squeezes my knee. I can't help but flit my gaze to the doomed building across the street. Sadness engulfs me, but I clasp Uncle Mars' hand and try to smile before I exit the car. My mouth doesn't cooperate.

Oliver stands still as a statue by the monkey bars with the strangest look on his face, watching the red Jeep drive away. A tumultuous cloud of emotion swirls across his features, his mouth set in a slash. When I approach, he shakes out his limbs and empties his skateboard from his backpack, the entire mood shifting in the blink of an eye.

"I put new wheels on and I want to break them in," he announces. He flips the board in his hands and unfolds it to its full length. Sure enough, neon green wheels glisten like polished gems underneath. Oliver sets the board gently on the ground before letting out a whoop and pushing full-tilt off the pavement. He speeds around the playground with each pump of his leg, picking up momentum before leaping over a set of steps with a bend of his knees. Exhilaration ripples through me like a warm breeze, and I clap and stamp my feet as he steers the board back to start. His mastery with the skateboard mirrors how I've practiced my cursive. The smallest details matter—so you don't fall flat on your face.

"Do you want to try?" Oliver asks, his voice breathy. The glint in his eye lights me up inside. Glancing over at the library, the light in me glows brighter, fueled by anger at the injustice of it all. I can't believe I'm going to do this. But look where playing it safe has gotten me so far. Perhaps courage would be worth a shot to shake things up. Honestly, there's nothing left to lose.

Oliver dismounts the skateboard and shows me how to place my feet for the most stability. The second my shoe brushes the sandpapery surface of the board, doubt creeps into my mind. This will end with a trip to the hospital, I'm sure.

Oliver grabs my hand and braces me from the ground. I bite my lip and give him a quick nod. Here we go. Do or die.

He pushes from behind and I roll forward, flapping my arms to keep balance as my stomach churns. I'm rolling! My senses heighten. The playground teems with activity—grasshoppers launching across the lawn, children giggling down the slide, the call of geese from a southbound V. I toss my head back and the adrenaline washes over me in a surge. Oliver jogs along the side of the skateboard and I'm emboldened by pure thrill. I balance on one foot and lower the other to the cement, making a quick succession of kicks to gather speed. My loops can't keep up. I'll leave them in the dust. Everything blurs around me in an abstract painting.

Which is why I don't see the tree.

The skateboard catches on a twisted root next to the sidewalk, and I somersault through the dirt with a yelp, scraping my elbow before landing face down on the earth.

Oliver is next to me in a flash. "Maybelline, are you alright? I shouldn't have let go. Can you stand?"

Shoulders quivering, I twist around and lose myself to uncontrollable laughter. Bright, twinkling squeals rebound off the branches above and back to my ears. Tears gather in my eyes and my breath escapes me, not from pain, but joy. My laugh sounds foreign, as if it belongs to a stranger. I wonder what my voice would sound like if I spoke.

Oliver reaches down to help me up, but I grab his hand and pull with all the force I can muster. He tumbles to the grass with an oof and a grin. *Now we're even,* my eyes tell him. Oliver blushes and turns away.

"I like when you laugh. It reminds me of someone I used to know," he mumbles before crawling to retrieve his skateboard.

Heat dapples my cheeks and I stand to stare unblinking at the library.

Unlike Mama, the library is still here. Which means there's still time to change what happens. With the energy coursing through me, I feel like I could move mountains. I don't know how, but I'm bound and determined. Skateboarding has unlocked a new, unshakeable Maybelline. Nothing and no one can stop me.

I'm going to save the library.

Chapter 26

BOUNCING FROM FOOT TO foot, I wiggle while I wait for Oliver to collapse his skateboard and store it away so I can drag him by his hoodie sleeve in the direction of my house. Time to enact Operation Save the Library: Phase One...bringing Oliver up to speed.

We fly through the front door and up the stairs, and I whisk Oliver into my room and shut the door to guard from prying eyes. I don't want to lose the precious energy flowing through me, to crawl back in that deep, dark hole from when I found out my library was closing. No more waiting for catastrophe. Now's the time to make a difference!

I scoot my chair away from the desk and plunk Oliver down with a well-aimed push.

"Hey!" he exclaims and tries to stand back up. But I silence him with a single finger, then retrieve the crumpled newspaper from the waste bin and spread it across my desk. Oliver's eyebrows knit together while he studies the headlines. Pointing, I direct his attention to the library article.

His mouth forms an emoji O as he leans in to read the headline. Upon revisiting that heartbreaking title, shadowy strands of depression grab at my determination, but I squash them down with a strong harrumph. I'm done with sitting and stewing. In truth, I was done a long time ago. Time to *do* something.

You gotta take yourself seriously if you expect anyone else to do the same. Finally, Mama's saying something useful.

"It makes sense now," Oliver whispers, leaning back in

the chair and running a shaky hand through his curls. He sizes me up. "This is a major bummer. The library is super important to you."

I roll my eyes and clutch my whiteboard, cursiving like I've never cursived before. Once finished, I twist the board around with a smirk.

We're going to save the library.

Oliver bites his lip and looks at the article.

"The town council voted to build a new library. How can we change a vote that's already happened?" His words come out slow and stiff.

Old is just as good as new. We can think of something.

"Hmmmm." Oliver rotates back and forth on the chair. I plop onto my bed and we spend a few minutes lost in thought.

What if we fix it up so it's like new?

I know I'm drawing at straws, but Oliver's face brightens.

"I bet my dad could help. He's known the Campbells for a long time. Plus, the library's where he had his first date with my... " Oliver fades away, tugging and twisting on his hoodie string. "I'll ask him."

In the meantime, is there something WE can do???

Important questions deserve *three* question marks.

That's it! I leap from my seat and toss the whiteboard into Oliver's lap to take a victory jog around my room.

"Umm, earth to Maybelline. What's the plan?"

We'll write an article about the library and why it should stay open. We can ask everyone in town for reasons and support!

I write so fast that my cursive turns to squiggles, so it takes Oliver a minute to decipher the message.

"Genius!" He leaps to his feet.

I grab his hands and we do a celebratory dance. A little warning bell goes off in the back of my mind when I realize how close we are, practically inches apart. He's got freckles dotted across his nose.

I clear my throat and throw him a smile.

Before he leaves, Oliver promises to come up with new questions for our article so we can start the interviews tomorrow. A warm bubble of hope envelops me and carries me through the rest of the evening. Even Lyla's snide remark at dinner about my new "boyfriend" rolls off my back.

I'm so hyped up that at bedtime, I cannot sleep a wink. After an hour of tossing and turning, I flip on my bedside lamp and fetch *Walk Two Moons* from my backpack. Reading is my version of a glass of warm milk.

Salamanca's friend, Phoebe, has also lost her mother. Salamanca keeps her feelings to herself, but Phoebe's anxiety is plain to see. The two kids remind me of Oliver and myself, which gets me thinking...perhaps I'm more like Phoebe, directing my anxiety on the situations around me. She makes up some wild stories and accusations. Is that how people see me when I lose my cool?

Drifting to the twilight space between asleep and awake, Oliver appears in my mind's eye. That would make Oliver Tree Hiddle the main character, the boy with the mysteriously absent mother. What happened to her? Did she leave or pass away? And why doesn't he talk about her?

Sleep comes stealthily, and my unanswered questions dangle like stars in the night sky.

****

A chilled autumn breeze nips my ears at drop-off the next morning, and I hurry, hunched, into the school. Most of the students are milling in the giant entryway before class. The high ceiling channels the noise upwards until it echoes. I'm reminded of the time we visited a museum over spring break, with hordes of families mingling together, small children zipping every which way. Younger Maybelline didn't like the crowds, especially when that rude teenaged boy shoved past to take a picture of one of the exhibits with his phone. Somehow, crowds don't hold the same power over me now. I take a deep breath in and smile.

A familiar bossy voice cuts through the chatter, and I spot Lyla's purple coat positioned in the middle of a large group of students. She's standing on a short ledge, waving a packet of papers above her head. I slink closer. What could she be up to? The steely glint in her eyes pulls my interest.

"It's our responsibility to make a difference! Thousands of helpless animals are used for food every single day. It's time to speak up so the school stops serving meat! Save the animals!" Lyla hands her packet to the nearest student, and immediately the kid scribbles down his name. She watches the papers progress around the circle with a smirk. Friends chatter to each other and I catch snippets of conversations. "Cool!" "Smart!" "Exciting!" They're eating out of the palm of her hand.

Leave it to Lyla to get radical. At this rate, we'll be eating salads on hot lunch days. Still, I have to admit she's pretty inspirational. I don't know another thirteen-year-old who would fight for what she believes in.

Wait a second.

A petition! That's the answer. That's how we'll save the library. I bounce up and down right in the middle of the school entryway. Lyla notices me and rolls her eyes. But even her blasé attitude can't ruin my mood. She's a mastermind! Pushing through the crowd, I approach Lyla and brandish my blue clicky pen, ready to get a closer look and sign her petition. She crosses her arms when I draw up beside her. If looks could kill, I'd be a bona fide ghost.

"Maybelline." She greets me with a suspicious glare.

I wave my pen before her nose and take my turn signing the document.

"Going vegetarian?" Judgment drips from her every word.

I grin in return. Library journal to the rescue. I scrawl the message,

I didn't know you started a petition.

Lyla's eyebrows rise and she side-eyes me. "You never asked," Lyla grumbles. "Why the sudden interest?" She places her hands on her hips and I craft a response.

Where did you learn how to write a petition?

Her eyes narrow into little slits. "My friend Peter. His dad works for the city council and his mom's a lawyer."

Do you have a blank copy?

"Not with me. I'll tell you what. How about I print you a copy at home?" Lyla's smirking again now.

My stomach twists as I wait for the 'but'.

"But, you'll owe me a favor." There it is.

Like what?

"I'm not sure. I'll figure it out." Lyla carefully slips the signed petition into her sticker embossed folder. A warning bell blares, and the mass of students begins to disperse.

Lyla's going to hold this over my head for a long time. But what else can I do? I need to know how to make a petition.

Deal.

I scribe, and we seal the pact with a quick handshake. Goosebumps prickle up my arm from Lyla's clammy palm. Will I regret this later?

"Have a good day!" Lyla says and struts away.

The hair on the back of my neck stands on end. Why does it feel like I just made a terrible mistake? I shake out my shoulders and head to class, glancing behind me every now and again expecting to see Lyla stalking me.

****

Oliver presents me with a sheet of paper the moment my bum hits the stool in science.

"Check it out! A+ on last week's math quiz! All thanks to you!" His smile stretches from ear to ear, and for a second, I'm caught in the sparkle of his planetary eyes. Shifting uncomfortably, I hold the paper over my face like I'm scrutinizing his quiz. Has Mrs. Quark turned up the thermostat? I hand the paper back to him with a thumbs-up, my cheeks flushed with heat.

"Are we kicking off the interviews today?" Oliver whispers behind his hand as Mrs. Quark calls the class to order.

I've got a better idea.

Oliver's forehead scrunches at the note.

I'll explain later. But it will change everything, I'm sure of it.

"You can't leave me on that kind of cliffhanger!" Oliver teases.

I sense a presence behind us and flip around. Mrs. Quark stares and motions to our textbooks. Dutifully, Oliver and I leaf through the pages. She heads back to her desk.

After school, I mouth. *I promise.*

Oliver sticks out his tongue, but his eyes keep grinning. We throw ourselves into our schoolwork, but I'm buzzing inside like a hive full of bees ready for spring. Blossomed hope tastes honey-sweet.

Chapter 27

I'll meet you at the library.

I PASS OLIVER THE note on the way to our lockers after the final bell. He opens his mouth to object, but I sprint away from him down the hallway.

"Hey, no fair!" he shouts, but doesn't pursue.

Someone must have plugged me in and turned me on high because I urge Uncle Mars to drive faster toward our house and vibrate where I sit, even though I know Lyla will take longer riding home on the bus.

Pacing back and forth inside the front door, I glance beyond the curtains for that tell-tale flash of yellow. After forever minutes, the bus screeches to a halt on the corner and Lyla hops out. Tracking her progress down the sidewalk, I nibble my pinky nail even shorter.

"Maybelline, do you want a snack?" Uncle Mars asks from the kitchen.

I pop my head through the doorway and shake emphatically NO. Uncle Mars laughs, disassembling a cracked cell phone on the table. He starts tinkering with the insides as the front door flings open.

Lyla has earbuds in, and her fingers fly across her phone, face illuminated by the bright screen. She drops her backpack and leans against the nearest wall, oblivious to me. I snatch away her phone without a second thought.

"HEY!" she snarls through gritted teeth. "Give it back."

I blink at the sparkly purple phone resting in my palm. What am I doing? I need Lyla's help, not more friction. I place the phone into her waiting hand. She glares at me, but her taut shoulders loosen. That phone means *wayyyy* too much to her.

I hold my hands palm up between us, keeping my face as expressionless as possible. She rolls her eyes and digs into her backpack, pulling out a wrinkled sheet of paper.

"Turns out you can print at school using the Wifi." She shrugs, dropping the paper into my grasp. Victory! I fold the petition template into even squares and store it in my pocket, making for the door.

Lyla braces her arm against the door jam and I smack my nose on her elbow.

"We made a deal," she whispers, gaze flicking to the archway leading to the kitchen.

Uh-oh. This can't be good. I clench my jaw and fiddle with a strand of hair.

"I want you to convince Mom and Dad to let me go to the Halloween dance... with a date." Lyla's words are so muted that I would have bet she'd also taken a vow of silence. I almost snort at her absurd request. The Thompson family's got a strict policy on dating. According to Uncle Mars, "no boys until you're married." But when I lock eyes with Lyla, I notice the desperate scrunch to her eyelids, the way her mouth droops into a dejected frown. Against my better judgment, pity rises in my chest.

"They trust you way more than they trust me. If you back me up, they'll probably agree." Her words flow faster than soft-serve ice cream in the hot sun.

Sighing, I extend my hand. *Bad choice, Maybelline. You're just getting her hopes up.* But I can't say no; I made a deal. Lyla pulls me in for an awkward hug, swinging me around in an exaggerated loop. As soon as she releases me, I'm out the front door and en route to the library.

****

As I meander up the front sidewalk, I envision a reality in which the library no longer exists—just a stretch of empty space and barren dirt remaining, like a grave. Shivers travel down my spine and I tie my hair into a messy ponytail. Not if I can help it. Oliver scuffs across the library's wooden porch, hands stuffed into his back pockets. I spy Cuddles on the nearest rocking chair, yellow eyes fixed to Oliver's movement. A weighted silence cocoons the library like a false protective shield.

"What took you so long?" Oliver asks, swinging from the closest rafter. Cuddles hisses softly and Oliver releases the wood, eyeing the cat with a glance.

I mime a conversation by opening and shutting my hands.

"Har, har," Oliver says. But he holds the front door open for me with a small smile. Cuddles follows us in, brushing like black velvet against my ankles. I almost forget to drop a penny into my wishing bucket but promptly double back. As the coin hits the water's surface, I scrunch my eyes shut and wish so loud I'm sure the whole world can hear me.

I wish this library will never go away.

Once inside, I'm greeted by an extraordinary amount of light. All the dark corners and crevices of forgotten shelves come into focus as I peer, squinting, around my most cherished safe place. Mrs. Campbell stands at the base of a green ladder, gaze angled up as she chats with someone out of view. Oliver grins, arms crossed, observing my reaction. I hold my hands up to the ceiling and draw a question mark with my forefinger. What's going on? Has Mr. Campbell returned?

A few steps further and I recognize the figure on top of the ladder. Mr. Grant, Oliver's dad! He's stretched toward the ceiling with wires dangling from his fist like streamers. A new chandelier hangs lopsided from a high beam. My smile cracks my face wide open, and I hop up and down, delighted.

"Surprise!" Oliver bellows. I expect Mrs. Campbell to shush him. We're in a library after all, but she waves us closer with a sparkle in her eye.

"Maybelline, you continue to amaze me!" Mrs. Campbell sighs, pulling me in for a long hug. My eyebrows arch at Oliver lurking behind Mrs. Campbell. He clears his throat.

"Dad's going to help however he can to get the library in tip-top shape," Oliver explains, rifling through his dad's brown toolbag and passing him a screwdriver.

"Gotta have some good light for reading," Oliver's dad mumbles around a couple of screws pressed between his lips. Relief massages the knot in my back. That tiny spark of hope feeds off the extra air in my lungs and grows into a full-fledged flame.

"That ought to do it for now." Oliver's dad descends the ladder and claps his hands to his pockets before packing the tools into his bag. "I'll stop by tomorrow to take a look at your roof leaks. Oliver, see you for dinner."

Mrs. Campbell escorts Mr. Grant to the entryway and Oliver trails me over to the computers. I play with my pen while the screen comes to life, clicking a fast-paced tune. Oliver scratches his head.

"So what's this all about?" he asks, spinning his hoodie string around his finger. He's so close that his body heat tickles my cheek, but now the nearness soothes my nerves instead of fraying them. We're in this together, through thick and thin.

I hand him Lyla's crumpled petition and his eyes go round as skateboard wheels. Brow furrowed, the missing puzzle pieces fall into place. He nods his head as he reads.

"You're onto something. I've seen petitions online that have gotten thousands of signatures," Oliver says.

Finally, the computer buzzes to life. I open a Word program and swipe the petition from his grasp to use as an example.

"Well, let me help," he grumbles. Side by side, we craft a new petition specific to our plan. Oliver makes adjustments to the words as he reads aloud, and I type like my life depends on it.

SAVE SALEM PUBLIC LIBRARY PETITION
All Salem Residents and Government Officials: This is a petition to support the preservation of Salem Public Library so it may continue serving the town in the future. Books make the world better and the library has helped readers of all ages since 1920.

Please sign below if you'd like to save the library for the sake of readers everywhere.

Before hopping to my feet, I add a bunch of lines to the bottom of the document for signatures. I've brought an entire pocket worth of pennies and run jingling over to the front counter so Mrs. Campbell can exchange a dollar's worth for dimes. Each printed paper will cost ten cents, so we have enough money for ten pages. Oliver crams in a few more lines for signatures on the page and then I press print.

"Do you think this will work? We're gonna need a ton of names to get noticed," Oliver says.

I throw him my best Lyla glare and his mouth snaps shut. We cannot fail. The library needs us.

Once we've stapled together hot-off-the-printer pages, Oliver sneaks off to the government section of the library searching for additional information on how petitions work.

Once he disappears in the stacks, I click on my Gmail account. Zero inbox messages only slightly deflates my enthusiasm, but I brush off my sadness to open a new blank message. I'll fill Mama in, and she'll be so proud that she'll call me as soon as she reads my email. I imagine if she created a petition, it would get a million signatures. She never takes no for an answer. My stomach churns as I type and hope that I can channel my inner Mama into this new project, while not losing myself in the process. How much of me is like Mama, anyway? A pit forms in my belly the more I think about it. I can't decide if our similarities make me happy or afraid. Is it possible for those similarities to just... exist? Do they have to be good or bad?

Dear Mama,

I've got big news. There was a newspaper article that said the library would close, so I'm teaming up with a friend to save it. This is my biggest adventure yet. Do you have any ideas on how we can keep the library open? You always have the best ideas. I miss you a lot, but when you come visit I'll show you the library for sure.

Love you, Mama.
Your Maybelline

Chapter 28

THURSDAY AFTER SCHOOL I'M itching to gather signatures, but Aunt Julie says therapy comes first. We don't have time for silly delays, but I know my Aunt won't budge. There's no use in arguing. Aunt Julie picks me up from school and I wiggle in the back seat while she chatters about the new braces options at work. I clamp my hand around the petition, and I can't help but skim over the wording for mistakes. Neatness matters. No one will take a pair of kids seriously unless the petition is perfect. Swallowing a wad of saliva, my heartbeat quickens as worst case scenarios run rampant through my brain.

Kids laughing at us.

Adults ignoring us.

Salem residents not caring about the library.

Me losing the library forever.

Fishing out my yellow smiley face ball, I give it a rapid series of squeezes and rest my forehead against my other palm. Getting worked up doesn't help anything. Anxiety paralyzes me, makes me useless. I hate worrying all the time, being afraid when I should be confident, composed, and in control... like Mama. By the time we enter the therapy waiting room Aunt Julie's gone silent, as if my bad mood has sucked the air right out of the building.

"Welcome, Maybelline! Come on in!" Miss Mendoza glides to her chair and I close the office door behind me. Her tangy citrus perfume clears the dark fog in my head. Gotta get through therapy so I can start collecting signatures. Easy-peasy.

"How was your week, dear, on a scale of 1 to 10?" Miss Mendoza flips open my folder, pen at the ready. I nearly laugh at the question. There's way, way too much to explain in one sitting. So I just shrug.

"Mm-hmm." Miss Mendoza taps a finger to her chin. "Let's stay in the now. Would you like to meditate, draw, or write? What are you feeling today?"

For a moment, my crimped golden hair falls between us like a wall. Huffing, I tie it into a ponytail and out of the way. I want to work on saving the library.

Wait a second. That's it. Petition work starts now.

I'm on my feet and to the doorway before Miss Mendoza can blink, ripping the door open and sprinting straight to Aunt Julie's purse. Slipping a hand in the side pocket, I snag her keys and jog to the car.

"Maybelline, slow down. What's going on?" Aunt Julie frantically chases me, Miss Mendoza at her heels. A twinge of guilt tugs at my heart. Quickly, I grab my backpack and toss the keys back to Aunt Julie. The tension melts from the grown-ups. Did they think I was going to drive away? I may be broken, but I'm not unhinged.

We head back to our respective seats. Miss Mendoza watches me with eyebrows tucked together, concern etched in the rigid corners of her mouth. Instead of trying to explain, I pull out the petition and extend the packet to her. She reads in complete quiet but for the whirr of the perpetual white noise machine.

She places my folder and the petition on her end table, drumming her pink manicured nails against the wooden surface. I take out the pen Oliver gave me, click it once, and pass it over.

Without a word, Miss Mendoza leans over the petition and signs her name in flourished cursive, right on the top line. Big bold beautiful strokes that bring tears to my eyes. She comes to sit next to me on the couch.

"This is an enormous goal you've set," Miss Mendoza begins, folding her hands in her lap. "I'll support you the best I can, but know that we only have control over ourselves." She reaches out her hand, palm up, and waits. With a deep breath, I extend my own and give her palm a squeeze.

Our hands together bring a memory to the surface.

Mama holding my hand to cross the busy street, her pink shimmery nails glistening like jewels. I asked every day to get my nails painted, and she finally took me for my fifth birthday. I chose gold sparkles, and she asked the technician to put little sunflowers on my thumbnails. *My favorite flower,* Mama said. I thought she meant the nails, but she was looking me in the face when she said it.

The memory fills me up until I'm sure Miss Mendoza can spot the happy glow radiating from my skin.

"Food for thought," she says abruptly, releasing my hand and going back to her chair. "In the middle of every month, the local government hosts a public meeting at the town hall. Residents attend and speak their concerns. It may be the perfect time to present your petition."

I blink and ponder her words. That would give us only a week to gather signatures, but it's the best shot for getting our petition noticed. Oliver and I can work together on a speech that he'll deliver. We can talk some sense into the town council. My breathing quickens as the excitement rushes through me. Miss Mendoza is a genius. I could leap across the room and hug her.

We end the session with deliberate breathing, but my mind stays in overdrive. The melodic chime that signals each breath also cheers me onward. *Think grander,* it whispers, *keep going.* The final note echoes within the depths of my heart long after the session concludes: *Yes, you can.*

Chapter 29

OLIVER HAS A FUTURE in sales. That kid can talk.

We arrive at school early on Friday morning and position ourselves near the glass doors, catching students as they enter. Man, am I glad that I have Oliver beside me, because otherwise I might faint again. Luckily, I remembered the extra pens and clipboard and busy myself with high-fiving anyone who takes the time to scribble a signature on one of our lines—even the boys. I guess in that way I'm courageous too. Breaking rules tests my bravery.

"The library has been around for a hundred years! I've spent time there myself, and legend says the building is haunted! Imagine a ghost helping you pick your next book. Super cool!" Oliver embellishes but keeps his face serious. Whispers and gasps ripple through the crowd. Students make a line to sign the petition, and I greet each of them with a broad smile. By the time the pack disperses to their classrooms, adrenaline surges through me. Blood rushing through my ears, we take a few minutes to review the petition. We've managed to collect two whole pages of signatures this morning! Oliver whoops and leaps into the air. When he lands, I punch him playfully on the shoulder and give him a giant hug. He's earned it. His curls brush against my forehead, soft and reassuring.

"Not a bad start, huh?" he nudges me with an elbow. My cheeks hurt from smiling, but I honestly can't stop. We're really doing this. And we might succeed.

"So we've got about a week until the town meeting, right?" Oliver gives me the clipboard and I nod, tucking the petition in my backpack for safe keeping. A warning bell blares and we tread down the nearest hallway together, footsteps light as if we're walking on air. I've completely missed my check-in with Mrs. Nightingale, but I'm sure she'll understand. I vow to stop by her office during my free period. Oliver places a hand on my shoulder.

"...the movie theater, the shopping center, Mario's, the recreation center, the aquarium. Am I missing anything?" Oliver asks.

I blink and tap a finger to my scalp, brainstorming. Inspired, I point to myself and mimic writing. Somehow Oliver interprets correctly. I'll write a list of the places we need to visit over the weekend. He gives me a thumbs up as we head into English, my loops are at full-tilt but actually productive for once. Oliver's dad should have plenty of time to spruce up the library, which we can mention in our speech for the meeting. And with how persuasively Oliver approached our classmates with the petition, I have no doubt he'll be able to handle talking to a bunch of grown-ups.

Each consecutive class passes as if I'm reading two books at once, with my focus split between paying attention to the lessons and working on the list for Operation Save the Library. When I exit the school, my spine tingles from the constant pumping adrenaline, but there's an optimistic skip in my step. Oliver and I agree to meet at Mario's Pizza at sun-up to launch our plan.

Uncle Mars' red jeep gleams like a mirror, and I catch a glimpse of myself in the reflection. My ponytail hangs cock-eyed from the side of my head, and I've got a smudge of pencil rubbed across my chin. At first I was disappointed we couldn't work on the petition because of family dinner on Fridays, but a tiny part of me knows I need a break before tomorrow.

Just before we pull away, the other back door opens and Lyla bounces into the car.

"Great to see you!" Uncle Mars exclaims. "No bus today?"

"It's faster going home with you guys. I can't wait for family dinner. Chinese is my favorite," Lyla says, her voice suspiciously upbeat. "Besides, it's been too long since Maybe and I have hung out."

Lyla drapes her arm around my shoulder and pulls me

close enough I can count the sparkles in her violet eye shadow. Sweat beads at the back of my neck. What is she up to? Uncle Mars and I frown in unison.

"Huh. Well, this is a nice surprise..." His eyes flit to the rearview mirror, but for once the concern is directed toward Lyla.

Lyla grins stiff as a porcelain doll until he turns up the radio, then she locks eyes with me in a mini staring contest. A sinking feeling of dread creeps across my chest as I remember our last conversation. *The favor.* She smirks at me. My loops spin faster the closer we get to home. Lyla puts in her earbuds and shuts her eyes, tapping her Converse sneakers against the center console to the beat of her mystery tune, which is probably the theme to a horror movie. Each tap deepens my eerie sense of foreboding.

****

"Please pass the veggie lo mein. And some sweet and sour sauce. Thanks." Lyla dabs her mouth with her napkin.

I roll my eyes. Talk about role reversal. But Uncle Mars and Aunt Julie are eating up her charade, which absolutely blows my mind. The last time Lyla used please and thank you, she still slept with a night light. Sure, they may be happy about her resurrected manners, but the fact that she hasn't once looked at her phone should be a major red flag.

"Sweet and sour!" Lucy exclaims through a mouth stuffed with rice. "Like me and you, Lyla!"

I nearly choke on my eggroll when I snort, and Lyla stiffens. Lucy pokes her chopsticks straight into her food instead of following the directions to pinch. Aunt Julie promptly fetches a fork.

Lyla grits her teeth, but smiles at Lucy. "Good one, Luce," she quips, monotone.

A sharp pain courses through my shin as Lyla kicks me under the table and clears her throat.

"So, I'm thinking of signing up for the dance committee this year," Lyla begins, sliding a saucy piece of broccoli back and forth across her plate.

"How exciting!" Aunt Julie responds.

Uncle Mars seems preoccupied with Lucy. He's inserted his chopsticks into his mouth like tusks but angled himself so Aunt Julie can't see. Probably better that he's distracted. He won't be happy with where this chat ends up.

"The Halloween dance is only a month away," Lyla continues serenely. "As a member of the committee, I'm required to go. Maybelline's going with me. Aren't you, Maybelline?"

I lose my grip on my egg roll and it plunks in some soy sauce, splashing droplets over the tabletop. *Breathe, breathe, breathe.* This was *not* part of the deal. I'm so mad I might spit fire. Pinching my lips together while I sop up the mess, I give a single nod of agreement.

Aunt Julie stares at me like I've grown a second head. "Of course you and Maybelline can go to the dance. What a great idea! Don't you think so, Mars?" Aunt Julie grabs Uncle Mars' sleeve and pulls him into the conversation.

"Sure!" He makes his voice deep-throated and spooky. "Have you thought about costumes?"

Lucy squeals.

"Maybe and I have way different styles." Lyla waves the suggestion away like a gnat. I fight a frown. "Would it be cool if I shopped for the dance with one of my friends, so we can get matching costumes?"

Uncle Mars' expression darkens. "Would this friend happen to be a boy?"

The entire kitchen stills. Even Lucy gets quiet, watching like a little owl as she crunches her crab rangoon.

"Nope!" Lyla peeps. "You've met my friend Sam, right? She's in my art class and totally cool."

It takes me a minute to catch up, but my loops finally put two and two together. Lyla said she wanted to go to the dance with a date... and now she's taking her friend Sam. Does that mean Lyla... likes girls? My mouth drops open, and I take a quick slurp of ginger ale to hide my shock. How did I not realize Lyla likes girls? Why won't she tell her mom and dad the truth? The fizzy drink churns in my stomach, followed immediately by a nervous burp.

Lucy laughs and the spell breaks.

"Good," Uncle Mars replies. "Because boys are absolutely off-limits until you get married."

"Yeah, yeah, Dad. Old news." Lyla digs into her lo mein with vigor.

The rest of my food goes cold while I process this new development.

****

On the way to the bathroom before bed, I bump into Lyla in the upstairs hallway and flinch, expecting the typical "Watch it" or "Get out of my way." Instead, she smiles a real Lyla smile, reminiscent of years past when we would build forts out of couch cushions or have competitions to see who could catch the most fireflies.

"Thanks," she whispers and shuffles away to her room without a backward glance.

Has the world turned upside down? Change usually makes me anxious, but right now I'm comfy-cozy inside and wondering where we'll go from here.

Chapter 30

OLIVER AND I MEET in front of Mario's Pizza at sunrise, the earliest I've been up on a Saturday since ummmm... ever. I took the liberty of drawing a map of our route so we can optimize the number of petition signatures we collect. Bouncing from the car in excitement (or from my sugary jelly-filled donut), I shield my eyes from the bright rays of sunlight streaking over the horizon. Oliver leans against the restaurant's brick wall, eyes closed and chest rising and falling in slow motion, as if he's napping. When I slam the car door, he pops upright with an enormous yawn.

"Sup?" he mumbles as I approach. A light breeze could knock him over.

I give him a playful shove, giggling, and he wobbles where he stands.

"What?" Oliver grumbles. "I'm not a morning person."

He claps his hands against his cheeks to wake himself up while I retrieve the petition from my backpack. Mario's doesn't open until noon, but Luigi, the owner (coincidental, I know) starts cooking before dawn. Sweet and tangy marinara sauce aroma wafts from behind the restaurant, and I pull Oliver after me to the back door. The thick metal door is propped open with an empty milk crate and my mouth waters as we approach. *Eyes on the prize, Maybelline. Don't let the most delicious pizza in the world distract you.*

After a soft rap on the door, heavy footsteps approach, and I shove Oliver in front of me. He clears his throat as the door swings open.

"Morning, kids!" Luigi booms. "Do you need some help?"

He glances back and forth down the alley before ushering us inside. Gooey balls of uncooked dough line the countertops, waiting to be twirled into discs for his famous pizza pies. My fingers twitch and I almost poke one, convinced it would satisfyingly squish like a brand-new batch of Playdoh. Marinara sauce bubbles on the stove, making my stomach grumble.

"Morning, sir," Oliver wipes an eye with the back of his hand, words dragging.

I step on his toe and his eyes grow large as tennis balls. He grimaces and tosses me a glare. I flash my pearly whites around the hot kitchen. Just keep smiling.

"Maybelline and I are working on a petition to save the library, and we'd love to get your signature. Do you like to read?" Oliver leans toward Luigi and Luigi, in turn, leans closer. That's got to be a good sign.

"Sure do, my boy. Guess my favorite book." Luigi says.

"Ummmm..." Oliver clenches his jaw.

"Cookbooks!" Luigi bellows, before clapping Oliver on the back, nearly sending him sprawling into a tub full of cheese. Luigi scrawls his messy signature on a line between throaty chuckles, leaving a trail of flour where his palm presses to the paper. I almost cringe because neatness matters, but force myself to stay passive. A signature is a signature.

"Tell you what. Leave an extra copy with me and I'll chat with customers about your mission. Saturday's our busiest day. I bet I can get a ton of signatures." Luigi smiles broad as a breadstick.

"Wow, thanks a lot!" Oliver exclaims, handing him the petition to copy.

Before leaving the restaurant, Luigi gives each of us a hot mozzarella stick, fresh from the fryer. We burn our tongues, but nothing could take away from the happy energy flowing through me. What an awesome start to the day.

"Where to next?" Oliver asks, fanning his mouth.

I hand him my map and point to the grocery store. We'll make a big loop around the main part of Salem and end our expedition at the library. My hope is to have all the pages full of names by lunchtime.

"Lead the way, boss!" Oliver insists, gesturing to a nearby walking path.

And off we go.

****

Salem Public Market teems with a morning crowd, whether from it being the weekend or the special on baked goods, I'm not sure. I hesitate outside the sliding glass entrance doors, my breathing gone shallow and raspy, and Oliver doubles back once he realizes I'm not following him. The last time I went shopping was for school supplies, and Aunt Julie made sure the store wasn't crowded before herding us inside. A bead of sweat trickles down my brow as patrons young and old step around us to enter the grocery store.

"I can go on my own, if you want," Oliver says, frowning.

I whip my head back and forth, setting my jaw in a stubborn slash. Annoyance makes goosebumps dance across my skin. Not this time. The petition is too important. No way I'm gonna hide away from more potential signatures.

Taking a deep breath as if I'm about to cannonball into the deep end of Salem's public pool, I catch Oliver by the hand and pull us both across the threshold. We wade through the swirling eddies of energy and noise while my heart beats loud in my ears.

"We should probably talk to a manager first!" Oliver says, pointing to a nearby office sign.

Once we've gotten the manager's approval, we set to work combing the aisles for signatures. Naturally, starting with aisle one and working our way across the store. We quickly hit our stride: introductions, signature, repeat. Some of the weight lifts from my shoulders. The citizens of Salem don't disappoint—by the time we've circled back to the exit, we've collected three whole pages of signatures!

The pulsing in my ears has been replaced by a happy, electric adrenaline buzzing through my body. I could float and dance on the wind like a balloon. We exit the store and I give a triumphant twirl, nearly bumping into the display of scarecrows. I don't know how many signatures the town council will require to save the library, but the pages we've already collected are an impressive start. My grin's so wide my cheeks ache as Oliver unpacks his skateboard for a victory lap around the parking lot.

When he comes to a halt beside me on the sidewalk, he hands me the petition for safe-keeping, and without thinking twice, I exclaim, "Thank you!"

Oliver stumbles to the side and nearly falls to the ground while his skateboard rockets away down the sidewalk. I clap my hand over my mouth and my face turns ice cold, like we've been plunged straight into winter. Biting my lip, I store the petition in its designated folder and avoid Oliver's bewildered stare.

"You... just talked... to me..." he gasps.

Why couldn't you just keep your mouth shut? Mama scolds in the back of my brain. Guilt gnaws on my insides. Strike one against my talking rule—the most important rule. I expect storm clouds to gather ominously on the bright horizon. I'll probably get struck by lightning. But the sky stays clear, curse-free. I cock an eyebrow, grateful but still uneasy, my paranoia ramped up to a ten. No doubt something bad will happen because I talked.

When I risk a peek at Oliver, he's got his chin in his hand like that famous statue, the Thinker. His curls twist and roil in the breeze.

"You sound different than I expected. Not quiet or anything. Maybe you've got more to say than you thought." Oliver shrugs, but smirks as if I've given away some kind of secret.

I roll my eyes and gesture to the map in a desperate attempt to change the subject. All the while, my loops spin like a whirlpool, relentless and threatening to suck me into the deep darkness dwelling inside my heart.

My hand shakes as I point to the library on our map. Oliver nods and retrieves his skateboard without a word, as if sensing my sudden change of mood. We proceed in awkward silence, and I can't help but feel that eight spoken letters and two syllables have somehow changed absolutely everything. What will be the consequences for talking when I swore to never speak again? Have I ruined my chance at being reunited with Mama?

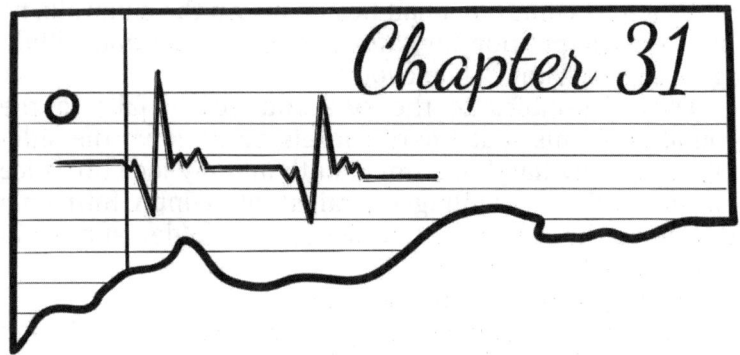

Chapter 31

MY FEET GROW HEAVIER with each step toward Salem Public Library, and by the time we mount the porch steps, the dread has settled like a cement block in my stomach and my mouth's gone completely dry. Gritting my teeth, I retrieve my long abandoned smiley face ball from the depths of my backpack and knead it like a wad of Luigi's pizza dough. We cross over the threshold and my lungs are tight. The sun's disappeared behind a thick cloud, and the usually inviting cubbies and corners inside the library seep with wispy shadows, black as night. I can almost imagine the shadows grabbing at me, snagging my backpack and dragging me away. I gulp, and Oliver motions me to the front desk, where Mrs. Campbell tip-taps upon her keyboard. Cuddles no doubt lurks in a cat-only hiding place. I wish I could too.

"Hello, kids! What can I help you with today?" Mrs. Campbell straightens her glasses, though her bun lays droopier than usual. Deep creases frame her eyes and mouth, like a sweater crumpled into a wrinkly mess. Luckily, her twinkly eyes remain bright.

"Well, ma'am, we've got some good news," Oliver announces cheerfully.

I procure the petition from my folder, handing it to Mrs. Campbell as heat tinges my cheeks. She reads slowly, and with each jump to a new line her eyelids open wider and wider.

When she's finished, she places the petition on the counter and regards us over the rim of her glasses. A flicker of pride sparks in my heart as she sits straighter on her stool, with the hint of a smile playing at the corner of her lips. Her twinkle shines brighter than before. We've helped already.

"I must say, I'm speechless and honored at your incredible efforts to preserve the library," Mrs. Campbell begins, running a hand through her disheveled hair. "Most days this place keeps me going, and I'm grateful to know it means so much to you."

Oliver grins from ear to ear, and I allow myself a shy smile.

"That being said, I want you kids to prepare for any outcome. Sometimes decisions are out of our control, and we have to roll with the punches." She must notice our faces fall because she plucks a pen from her nearby cup and signs her name at the bottom of the final page with a flourish.

I crane my neck to study her penmanship. Sure enough, her cursive scrawls compact and tidy, with each letter afforded the perfect amount of space for her entire name to feel balanced. A sigh of satisfaction escapes my lips.

Extending both her arms, Mrs. Campbell grasps our hands across the counter with a kind squeeze. "I believe in you... and I'm proud of you. You're both bound for a big future."

A tiny tear trickles from the corner of her eye down toward her nose and she wipes it away with a sniffle. Oliver hands her a tissue and I retrieve the petition, clutching it tightly to my chest, but not tight enough that it crinkles.

"Mrs. Campbell, is Mr. Campbell around? It would be great to get his signature on our petition too," Oliver asks a little too loudly, shifting on his feet.

Mrs. Campbell stares at us again over the rim of her glasses, before removing them entirely and placing them, folded, next to her computer.

Then she does something I wouldn't have expected in a thousand years.

Mrs. Campbell rounds her desk and heads to the front door, locking the deadbolt with a metallic click. In the middle of the weekend? During open hours? Oliver and I share a sideways glance, and she ushers us toward one of the lounge areas. My throat goes dry, undoubtedly an omen. *Breathe in, breathe out...* I remind myself while we wait. Mrs. Campbell fidgets on a wooden rocker, lacing her fingers together as if she's got a pair of knitting needles hidden in her palms.

"I've not mentioned these circumstances to anyone else, mostly because I've been processing recent events myself." She releases a heavy sigh and continues. "Over the summer, Mr. Campbell took a terrible fall. The doctors think he suffered a stroke, and he's been in the hospital ever since."

My hand flies over my mouth in shock, and Oliver sags in his chair. The library must have grown at least ten degrees hotter, because sweat breaks out at the base of my neck. My heart bump-bump-bumps in my ears. Mrs. Campbell continues her pretend knitting.

"I visit him daily in the hospital, but he's quite frustrated. He's lost some of his coordination and doesn't understand why he can't come home. I'm sorry to lay this on you kids, but you deserve to know the whole story... especially with your efforts to help our library." Now her hands ball into fists, trembling in the folds of her dress. Oliver's gone gray.

Why won't he say something? To my own surprise, I act without thinking. "I'm so sorry," I whisper, my voice outrageously loud in the library's stillness.

Standing abruptly, I offer Mrs. Campbell my open arms for a quick hug. She hesitates at first, but then pats me on the head and gives my hand another squeeze. Oliver stares off into the shelves, mouth locked in a grimace. We've swapped places, and I've dug myself a deeper hole. My loops spin frantic. I shove away the shame at having spoken twice in a single day. Mama doesn't have to know.

"I'm sure when I tell Mr. Campbell about your petition, it'll raise his spirits, no doubt," Mrs. Campbell strides back to the front door and unlocks the deadbolt, straightening her dress. "Thanks for listening, dears. Take all the time you need sifting through the books."

Mrs. Campbell tosses us a playful wink before perching behind her desk, all business. Oliver pops to his feet and paces through the rows of books. Chewing on the inside of my mouth, I wander toward the computers, my brain in a tailspin.

****

The stiff plastic chair digs into the back of my legs, hurt-

ing my tailbone as I swing my sneakered feet back and forth over the blue and white checkered tiles. A mechanical beep, beep, beep drones from the corner of the room, where a tangle of wires and machines prove that Mama is stable, at least for now. I try not to look at them or her, keeping my head down and counting the tiles stretched across the floor. Ten one way, twelve the other. The adults whisper just beyond the door, soft but frantic. My breath catches in my throat, and the bitter smell of antiseptic burns the inside of my nostrils.

Sneaking a peek at Mama, my hands tug a strand of my hair away from the rest, stroking methodically as I take in her discolored face and full arm cast. Mama's lip has swelled like a balloon, and she's got dark purple bruises on one eye and cheekbone. Her chest rises and falls more peacefully than it should, what with being in the hospital. Probably because they gave her so much medicine. Mama really likes medicine.

I desperately want to scoot next to the bed and wrap my fingers around her unbroken hand, but the twisting in my stomach holds me back. Mama got hurt and it's my fault. Tears drip onto a blue tile like raindrops rejoining the sea.

The creak of a door sounds behind me followed by a familiar voice. "Maybelline, can you join us in the hall for a minute?" Aunt Julie waits with a hand extended.

Blinking back the tears, I hop off my chair and tiptoe to the edge of the room.

"I'll be right back, I promise," I tell Mama before gently closing the door.

Aunt Julie waits with a lady in a dark skirt, matching jacket, and extra high heels. Despite her teetering height, the lady kneels to greet me, giving my hand a light shake. Her brow furrows ever so slightly, the way grown-ups look when they're worried. I've been getting that look a lot since yesterday.

"Maybelline, you've been through so much the last couple days, and I know that it'll take awhile for both of you to feel better. I'm sure the last thing you want is silly old me asking you a ton of... bothersome questions. However, it's important that you answer one question as honestly as you can." The lady's voice stays clear and she doesn't break eye contact. "Sweetheart, do you feel safe with your Mama?" she asks without blinking.

She's got the longest eyelashes I've ever seen.

Aunt Julie grips her hands together so tightly that her knuckles turn white. I stay quiet for a long time, thinking... wondering. Mama's taken care of me, but I don't know if that's the same as being safe. I bite my lip as images scroll through my mind. Mama red with fury over a broken vase. Mama slamming my bedroom door so hard the furniture shakes. Mama bringing strangers into our home and letting them stay. The recent slaps on my bottom that make it hurt to sit down. Wincing, I push the memory of the angry man away as tears pool again in my eyes. It feels like I'm letting Mama down by telling the truth. But she's always said, "Maybe, words have consequences." This conversation hums with such importance that I tremble where I stand. So, I answer the only way I know how.

"No."

Chapter 32

THE COMPUTER FREEZES AS it loads, so I punch the power button and restart the slow process of checking my email. I've lost myself to tracing the grains in the wooden desk with my finger when a sudden tap on my shoulder makes me jump. I swivel around and come nose to nose with Oliver. My heart races so fast that I can see the beat pulsing in my wrist. Let's chalk that up to nerves, not the flutter of something more in my stomach.

"Hey! Sorry to scare you. Are you ready to go? I've got to get some fresh air." Oliver still hasn't regained the color to his ashen cheeks, and his shoulders hunch as if bearing some invisible weight.

Shaking my head no, I catch a whiff of freshly mown grass. He's standing very close to me. *Play it cool, Maybelline. No big deal.*

"Tell you what, I'll wait out on the porch, and I can walk you home." Oliver fishes some earbuds out of his pocket and gives me a small smile before exiting stage left.

My loops spin quietly in the background, like white noise, as I consider his strange change of attitude. Ever since the chat with Mrs. Campbell, he seems… unsettled. My loops continue, even when I spin back around and the homescreen has finally appeared. Clicking into my email, the typical 0 new messages slaps me in the face, though my concern for Oliver has me distracted. I'll write Mama a quick message and hurry out to the porch to make sure he's all right.

Dear Mama,
Me again! You won't believe it. I figured out how to save the library! Lyla taught me all about petitions, so me and a friend are on a mission to collect as many signatures as possible. I've been thinking... if you come to visit, you could sign the petition and I can take you on a tour of Salem. I know you're really busy, but I miss you, Mama. Hope to hear from you soon!
Love,
Maybelline

And send! Before I can touch the big X to close my email, the inbox dings with a notification. My breathing goes shallow and my surroundings vanish as I register the hopeful 1 staring up at me from the previously empty inbox. Mama actually responded? And lightning fast too! Is she impressed with our petition plan? Does she want to help with Operation Save the Library?

Will I finally see her again after so long apart?

My hand flies onto the mouse and, trembling in anticipation, I position the cursor over the 1 in a flash. Taking a deep breath, I jab the button and an email pops up on the screen. The title reads in all caps "NOTICE." Scrunching my nose, I skim the message and my world disintegrates.

Sorry, we were unable to deliver your email to the requested address. The mailbox in question has been permanently closed.

Permanently closed?
PERMANENTLY closed?
Licking my lips, I taste salt. I'm crying... streams of tears cascade down my face, but my brain has stopped thinking altogether. I'm frozen like a computer screen. Someone ripped the cords of hope and optimism from my brain, leaving me unplugged and completely disoriented. Loops are bad, but this forever emptiness is worse.

I'll never talk to Mama again.

A strangled cry erupts from my mouth, and I have to get out. Get away. I snatch my backpack off the ground and sprint full force out the front door, screen door slapping against the library siding with a tremendous *BANG*.

"Maybelline! What's going on?" Oliver asks, but I don't stop... can't stop. If I stop running, I'll break into a million pieces right there on the sidewalk, to be blown away by the blustery autumn wind. Instead, I lean into my race, pushing even faster as the world swirls around me like a damp watercolor painting. My lungs sting in the absence of air, but I keep going, backpack slapping against my spine in frantic rhythm. Down the block, across the front lawn, up the fourteen stairs. My little room is my cage, so small that the walls press down on me as soon as I shut and lock the door.

Footsteps carry up the stairs and Uncle Mars calls out, "What's the story, kiddo?"

He jiggles the handle, but I wrench my desk chair to prop behind the door for extra support. Finally, I release my backpack to the floor with a thump.

That's when my loops rear their ugly head.

NOTICE.

Permanently closed.

NOTICE.

PERMANENTLY CLOSED.

My stomach jerks violently, and it's all I can do to grab my plastic wastebasket before the retching begins.

Chapter 33

DAYLIGHT TURNS TO DUSK, and the inside of my room fades to black with the setting sun. Having long since abandoned the gross wastebasket, my empty stomach roils with nausea though I'm lying perfectly still, curled upon my bed like a wilted flower. Whispers hum in the hallway, impossible to understand, but I know they're about me. Once or twice, a soft knock on the door interrupts my mulling. I never answer. My loops spin me into a tizzy and I'm paranoid that my family is plotting something behind my back. As much as I want to care, my body's gone numb from top to bottom. Those horrible letters, NOTICE, flash through my thoughts like a warning, glowing an angry red. Heavy, salty tears threaten to surface again, though my eyes have no moisture left to give. I've cried so long that they feel dry and swollen, that it hurts to even breathe.

I'm jarred out of my stupor by nature... an undeniable need for the bathroom. I don't know how many hours I've been holed up in my room, but my bladder has kept track. Crossing my legs, I wait until I hear the clank of dishes from the kitchen to crack open my bedroom door and sprint down the hall. After relieving myself, I wash my hands and take a quick look at my reflection in the mirror. My eyes have red rings around them, like a discolored raccoon, and I must have been chewing my lip because an enormous split has crusted into an ugly brown scab. Splashing some water on my face and drying the salt away with the hand towel, I peek again into the hallway to make sure the coast is clear.

Only it's not.

Lucy hunches on the top stair, thumb tucked into her mouth as she did in preschool. Her other hand tugs at the fibers of the carpet, plucking out loose threads and thrusting them down the stairwell like dandelion seeds.

"Luce, time for dinner!" Uncle Mars announces from downstairs.

Now or never... if I wait, my Aunt and Uncle may realize I've emerged from my room. They'll want to talk. I'm never talking again. Mama's gone forever. Hustling down the hallway, I keep my gaze on the ground and ignore Lucy's little "eep" as I cross the threshold of my room.

"Maybe... can I..." she begins, but my slamming door cuts her off.

A stab of guilt catches my breath as I turn the lock, but I reclaim my position lying on the bed, scrunching my eyes shut and praying for some of the hurt to leave.

Eventually, sleep takes me.

****

One of the hardest parts of being a kid is figuring out the difference between real and pretend. People are pretty complicated. Usually, dreams are easy to decode. Cars don't fly in real life, and I've never swam with crocodiles in the Everglades. But sometimes, even dreams can parallel memories so much that we forget we're asleep... for a little while.

I'm on the front porch, leaning against my suitcase with my hands over my ears. Someone has a bonfire going down the street. Sweet, woodsy campfire smoke pokes at my nose and makes me sneeze. What I wouldn't give for a s'more right about now. My mouth waters and I lick my lips. Furious voices erupt from around the corner of the garage.

"You have no right to make this kind of decision. Our life is none of your business," Mama spits, her tone deep as a growl, loud and dangerous.

"You know it wasn't up to me," Aunt Julie insists—her voice trembles and cracks like logs on a fire.

"So you say, but you and I both know the truth, Jules. You're a lousy liar." No doubt Mama's face has gone red, her fingernails digging into her palms. I don't need to see her to

picture her worst kind of anger.

A stem of worry sprouts in my chest, hoping she won't lash out at Aunt Julie. I know sometimes sisters fight, but I don't think my aunt fights ugly like Mama can. I press my hands harder against my ears.

A tap on my shoulder brings me to. Mama stands before me, tense as a coiled snake, a single tear tracking down her cheek. She brushes it away and pulls me up gently, by my arm. I've never known Mama to be gentle when she's mad. My heart sinks further into my chest.

"Baby, you're gonna stay here for a while," Mama starts, monotone. Her eyes burn with passion, but the rest of her remains perfectly calm.

"Are you staying too?" I clamp Mama's hand tight. She bends down and gazes straight into my eyes.

"Listen to your Aunt and Uncle. I better not hear about any sass." Mama taps the tip of my nose while I blink, confused. "Remember what I told you. Follow the rules... neatness matters."

"I don't want to stay here on my own. Where will you be? We should stick together," I whisper, mouth suddenly dry.

Mama frowns and turns her head away, sniffling twice before encasing me in a tight hug.

"Why couldn't you just keep your mouth shut?" Her bitter words brush against my ear before worming their way into my brain, and I remember my conversation with the lady at the hospital.

Mama knows.

Gasping, I try to pull away, but Mama holds me firm.

"Don't you ever forget me, Maybelline." And she laughs. A quick ruffle of hair, and Mama marches away, head held high and regal as a banished queen. Her car engine kicks on and she's pulled her sunglasses down over her eyes. The car's stinky exhaust makes me sputter. Then she's backing out of the driveway, maneuvering down the street and completely out of sight. I'm stuck on the porch, her final words twisting the very first infinite loop, trapping me inside my own head.

When we have nightmares, all we want is to wake up. Some lucky kids know when they're having a nightmare and can force themselves awake. Lyla used to do that when she had a bad dream about spiders or tornadoes.

Other kids aren't scared of nightmares... because their real life is worse. And there's no way to wake up from real life.

Chapter 34

STIRRING FROM SLEEP FEELS like dragging myself through a pool of mud. A dry crust of salt coats my eyelids and they stick together, compelling me to stay in bed. Upon closer inspection of my bedside alarm clock, I slip off my mattress to the floor. 12:45? In the afternoon? Aunt Julie let me sleep in on a school day? Is it the end of the world?

And then I remember. Mama. The email. My pulse quickens and I snatch my alarm clock, hurling it across the room. CRASH! It collides with the opposite wall and breaks into pieces. The thump of footsteps on the stairs follows shortly after. I stay where I am behind my bed, face in my hands, waiting.

But instead of a frantic knock, my door knob rattles. A metallic jiggling continues, and I realize too late that someone's picking the lock. The door swings open, flooding my hiding place with daylight. Aunt Julie's silhouette lingers in the doorway, and I spy a pair of hairpins in her hand. She's breathing hard.

"What in the world, Maybelline? Are you all right?" Her eyes flit to the busted alarm clock. "You scared me..."

Her worry transforms to a rigid stare when I don't respond, mouth setting into a stubborn line and shoulders stiffening. She marches to my curtains and throws them apart before wrestling open my dresser drawers and tossing clothes in my direction.

"Sweetheart, I've tried to be patient, but I'm in the dark here. I can't help you if you don't tell me what's going on."

Aunt Julie points a trembling finger in the direction of the bathroom. "Get dressed. We're heading to therapy."

The angry part of me wants to throw something else, but a remnant rational thought tells me this would be a horrible idea. So instead, I stomp to the bathroom and get ready as slowly as possible, inching my toothbrush across my teeth at a sloth's pace.

Aunt Julie's got the front door open wide, with her arms crossed and toe tapping against the hardwood floor. I take my time on the stairs, watching my feet like I'm afraid they'll move on their own. When I pass the kitchen, Uncle Mars gives a little wave, which makes me pause. Usually, tech dude stays in the zone. How worried are they? My stomach gurgles as we get in the car, and Aunt Julie hands me a snack bag of mini muffins. The drive remains deathly silent except for the crinkle of the bag as I empty it of the chocolate chip yumminess.

When Aunt Julie parks and shuts off the car, she turns around to look at me. My cheeks bulge with crumbly muffins, but I try to glower at her. She matches me, wrinkled brow for wrinkled brow, like I'm looking in a mirror.

"I called ahead so Miss Mendoza would know it's an emergency. Help me, Maybelline. Help us to hep you. We will not be leaving this office until I have a better understanding of what's going on. Do you hear me?" Her voice trips on the question.

The muffins turn to rocks in my belly. I nod, barely. I don't want to upset Aunt Julie, but I have no idea how I'm going to share my feelings right now. I'll never speak again, that's for sure. I don't even understand the emotions tangled up inside me. Lungs constricted, breathing shallow, I shadow Aunt Julie straight into Miss Mendoza's office.

Straight into the unknown.

****

Miss Mendoza remains kind and cheerful as ever, inviting us to take a seat on her fluffy couch and begin with some breathing exercises. My aunt sits next to me on the couch. I can't help but sneak a peek at Aunt Julie between inhales and exhales. Though she goes through the motions, there's a tension in her shoulders that keeps her perfectly straight.

Mama taunts me with *your fault.* My heart drops. She'd been in my head less often since we started the library petition. Why does this feel like ten steps backward?

"Now..." Miss Mendoza shuts off the calming instrumentals and swaps to her white noise machine.

Grabbing my knees with my hands, I wait, not breathing.

"It's normal during treatment to have ups and downs. In fact, that's a part of being human." Her lilting giggle punctuates the silence.

Aunt Julie cracks a small smile, but I continue staring straight ahead.

"Through this entire experience, we've established the most important stepping stone is communication. Maybelline, do you feel comfortable communicating with us today?" Miss Mendoza shifts into my line of view. I meet her eyes and hope she can read my mental SOS.

She does. "Clearly, something's unsettled you. So here's what we're going to do." Miss Mendoza retrieves two pads of paper and a couple of pencils from a basket by her desk. "I'd like you both to write a message to each other. You can say whatever you feel right now. Maybelline, you don't have to mention recent events that triggered you... unless you want to, of course. I'll give you some time to write your notes, and then we can swap and read aloud."

I flinch at the word "aloud."

Miss Mendoza knows me all too well. "I'll read your Aunt's note, Maybelline. You'll just need to listen."

Some of the pressure lifts from my shoulders as we grab our pencils to start. Aunt Julie doesn't hesitate, and she's already finished her first paragraph while I sit idle and nibble my pencil's eraser. With the snap of a lighter, Miss Mendoza sparks a new candle... Baja Breeze. The salty fresh aroma of the ocean wraps me in a warm hug, and I begin to write.

Aunt Julie,

I know I'm not the easiest person to care about. Trust me, I never wanted to make you worried or upset. It's so easy to get caught in the loops in my brain and forget that I've got family who aren't following along. I'm sorry for pushing you away. I know you love me and want to help, but I don't know what will help. I really miss Mama, even though I don't want to. And I'm worried I'll never talk to her again. I feel like there's something wrong with me, and that's why she won't contact me. Thanks for listening, Aunt Julie.

Love,

Maybelline

Rereading the note, it doesn't hurt as much as I expected. I haven't said anything specific, but Aunt Julie might have a better understanding now. That hope of having someone close to me who 'gets it' lifts me like helium in a balloon.

Miss Mendoza reads Aunt Julie's letter first. She must have erased some because it's shorter than the version I saw.

"Dear Maybelline,

I'm so lucky to be your aunt. I've watched you grow from a little girl to a brave middle schooler, and I've been proud of you every step of the way. I'm sorry if I don't tell you often enough that you inspire me. I remember when your Mama and I were kids. I loved her more than anyone else, even when she made it hard. Sometimes, I see glimpses of her in you... the way you laugh at a funny joke, or the expression you make when you concentrate. Parts of your Mama are special and good, even though she's hurt people through her mistakes. Just know that you aren't the only one who loves her in spite of her flaws, and that I will always be here for you no matter what. You can count on me. I promise.

Love always,
Aunt Julie"

I've never considered what it was like growing up with Mama... how her temper might have affected her relationships as a kid. Aunt Julie probably understands more than anyone else ever could. With a quick breath for courage, I snatch her hand from the couch beside me and hold on tight. She looks ten years younger in that very instant.

Aunt Julie takes my letter and reads it aloud. She has to stop a couple times to dab at her nose with a tissue. When she's finished, she kneels on the ground in front of me and gives me a big hug.

"Maybelline, sweetheart, you are so easy to love. You have no idea," Aunt Julie whispers. "I wouldn't change a single thing about you, and I'll fight anybody who says otherwise."

"I'm proud of you both for communicating so effectively," Miss Mendoza chimes in as Aunt Julie repositions on the couch. "Now, Maybelline, are you willing to share any information about what got you so upset yesterday?"

Pressing my lips together, I scribble a quick note on a new sheet of paper. Aunt Julie already heard that I want to talk to Mama. The secret emails won't be a surprise... and I don't think they'll make her mad.

I've tried to email Mama when I visit the library, but yesterday I got a message saying her account was permanently closed.

I can't write after those two words: permanently closed. My stomach somersaults with nausea.

Miss Mendoza nods as she reads my admission, and Aunt Julie's hand flies in front of her mouth. I fiddle with a strand of my hair and watch the aqua candle flicker and pop. Don't cry. It'll just make everything worse.

"Maybelline, your Mama is still an important part of your life. It's only natural that a kid would want to talk to the parent who raised her. Why don't we see if we can come up with a way to contact your Mama?" Miss Mendoza suggests, gaze shifting over to Aunt Julie.

A silence follows and Aunt Julie starts fidgeting. Miss Mendoza clears her throat, poking Aunt Julie into action.

"Maybe, you've been honest with me today, and I need to be honest with you." Aunt Julie starts slowly, but she won't look at me.

A shiver of fear cascades down my spine.

"When your Mama first dropped you off at our house, she didn't want to leave you. I stood firm on keeping you with us because the courts had decided. But that's not the end of the story." Aunt Julie exhales a big breath.

Goosebumps prickle along my arms.

"Your Mama tried to call you on a weekly basis, but I spoke to her instead, at the recommendation from the social worker. You had been through a tremendous ordeal, and we thought talking to your Mama might bring up some frightening memories. We thought with time you'd adjust to your new living situation and then we could let the two of you reunite, even through a phone call. But we were wrong." Aunt Julie clutches the edge of the couch like she might fall off.

"You stopped talking altogether, Maybe. And then you didn't want to go to school. I was at a loss. I couldn't tell your Mama about how you were doing because she would have tried to take you back... so I kept her calls a secret. I have her phone number in the safe at home. I'm so sorry, Maybelline. Don't you see you're not to blame for any of this? Your Mama has always cared about you too, even when she didn't know how to show it."

I'm frozen... stunned, processing, my fear switches to anger like the strike of a match. Lies upon lies upon lies. Here I'd thought Mama was the major manipulator in my life, but Aunt Julie has kept her away from me all along. The violent shaking starts from my toes and carries through my body, until my teeth are clacking together with rage. Aunt Julie's face has lost all color, and she leans back to give me space. A dark urge within me screams to push her hard, but I won't. I won't get physical like Mama. But that doesn't mean I have to trust Aunt Julie ever again. Crossing my arms, I turn my entire body away from her.

Miss Mendoza retrieves a squishy ball from her bookshelf (this one covered in peace signs) and hands it to me. I want to throw it back at her, but I don't. Instead, I scratch deep impressions through the foam with my nails. Can I trust anyone? Am I already completely alone?

"I think it's best if Maybelline and I continue the session with just the two of us, while she absorbs this information." Miss Mendoza leads Aunt Julie to the waiting room without a fuss.

The fire inside me grows into a roar, heat splashing across my skin like burn marks.

"Maybe, we're going to get in touch with your Mama. I know we can get your family on board, especially with Aunt Julie's explanation. You've come leaps and bounds from that little girl who didn't want to go to school." Her tone grows sharper, pulling my focus. "Don't let your instinctual reaction disregard the wonderful progress you've made. We'll try to sort through some of these feelings before the end of the session."

Using both trembling hands, I cup the squishy ball between my palms, dig in my nails, and pull with all the force I can muster. The halves completely sever with little resistance. Springing to my feet, I offer the ripped ball to Miss Mendoza. She takes the pieces and tosses them in her trash.

I sit in total silence until the hour's up.

Chapter 35

I PRETEND TO NAP on the way home, though Aunt Julie doesn't even try to break the invisible barrier between us with conversation. If she did, I might explode. When we pull in the driveway, I untangle myself from the seatbelt, leap onto the black top and slam the car door as hard as I can. Aunt Julie stays in the driver's seat, forehead resting motionless against the steering wheel.

Much to my surprise, when I lope around the car, I notice a figure sitting hunch-backed on our front stoop. Oliver. His skateboard lays upside down on his lap, and he twirls the wheels with his finger. He must sense me staring because our eyes lock and he's on his feet in a second, rushing over.

"Can we talk?" Oliver mumbles, eyebrows arched together like skate park ramps.

The fire still burns in my belly, and I desperately want to tell him no, but Oliver may be the last person in the world I should push away. He's earned my trust. Even thinking about him leaving gets me short of breath. So, I nod, and we climb the stairs together. I collapse on my bed and Oliver swivels the desk chair, inching closer so there's less than an arm's length between us. The butterflies flutter against my rib cage.

"When you didn't come to school, I got worried," Oliver begins. He's got his hoodie string wrapped around his hand already. I snag my white board hanging on the door knob and scrawl a quick reply.

I needed some space.

"Did I do something wrong?"

No. I had to sort through some stuff.

Oliver releases a long hiss of air then runs his fingers through his dark curls, his features softening into a grin. "Phew, that's a relief," he sighs. "We've gotten so far with the petition that I didn't want to screw anything up. Plus... you're kind of my best friend now."

Rolling the marker between my palms, I cap and uncap the top over and over again. *Snap. Snap. Snap. Snap. Snap. Snap*, stopping only when I pinch the skin on my pinky.

I've been hoping that Oliver would call me his friend since the first day we were paired up. But something deep inside me rings like an alarm, urging me to get away. Caring is dangerous. People will disappoint me. The loops return full force, so fast that the room spins, making me dizzy. There's no way around the next message.

You've been an awesome friend to me. But, things have changed. I'm not going back to school ever again.

He reads while I write, objecting immediately. "Maybelline, you can't give up now. You belong at school. How will I get through my classes without your help?" Oliver's smile wavers. "Plus, we're so close to saving the library. I know we can do it."

He's not going to let this go. But I've made up my mind. My heart can't stand any more hurt. I'm safer all alone.

There's no way we can save the library. We're just two kids. And I'm not going back to school. I won't.

Oliver springs from the chair and paces the room, throwing his hands in the air and whipping them back and forth.

"I'm not sure what's going on here, but if you explain, I might be able to help. That's what friends do." He stares hard at the carpet, then continues. "You've helped me a lot too, you know? I've been kind of a mess since... the accident and losing my mom. You've helped me refocus and get out of my head." Oliver jams his hands in his hoodie pocket and gazes back at me, pleading. "I don't know how to do sixth grade without you."

I'm paralyzed at the mention of his mom, like the word has transformed into the trigger for a grenade. I don't want to talk about moms. Not now, not ever. Fury from the therapy session bubbles over. We're done here. I write messier than I've ever written before.

GET OUT.

Oliver stumbles as if I've physically pushed him. Hurt, confusion, sorrow flash like lightning across his face. I bite back my regret and fight the urge to apologize, instead handing him the folder with the petition in it to drive my point home.

"You can't mean that. You're not even going to tell me the whole story?"

My Mama left me. I'm done talking.

He stares straight at me, jaw clenched. "I thought you were different. That you wouldn't bail."

Just leave me alone. This has been a waste of my time.

I hate how I'm treating him, but I'm so mad it burns me from the inside out. Oliver braces against the wall and his eyes swell with tears. He opens his mouth a couple of times, but nothing comes out. Rereading my message, a sinking feeling punches me in the gut. A memory long blocked constricts my lungs. I really do sound like Mama. I heard those exact words out of her mouth... a long time ago.

Oliver swings open the bedroom door and now his voice is shaking. "You were supposed to be my friend," he says, his voice choked into a harsh whisper, before stomping down the stairs and out of my life forever.

Fat tears stream down my cheeks. I use my comforter to dry them, before laying back down and drawing my knees to my chin.

I'm better off without friends. People will only end up betraying you.

Plus, he's way better off without me.

Chapter 36

MAMA IS IN THE SHOWER, and I'm in my room, feet hanging off the bed while I read my favorite book, Corduroy. A strange shuffling noise echoes down the hall into my bedroom, breaking my concentration. I tip-toe across the carpet.

Pressed against the doorframe, I lean through as far as possible to have a clear view of the living room. A dark hulking form, his back in my direction, hunches over something on the couch. I should lock the door and go back to my bed, but my feet carry me forward like they had a mind of their own. Soon, I'm right next to the angry man, taking a deep gulp of air and summoning my courage to peek around his shoulders. He's got Mama's wallet, and the contents litter his lap in haphazard confetti. Credit cards, paper money... even Mama's newest paycheck from her work. My stomach drops. Mama works hard for that money. He's stealing. Scrunching my forehead and squaring my shoulders, I clear my throat to get the angry man's attention.

"Ummmmm..." I mumble.

He spins to face me, and I'm hit with a blast of sour breath. His eyes droop and take too long to focus.

"Getttt..." he slurs, before turning back to his pile of goodies.

Balling my fists, I nudge him again.

"No. That's Mama's money. You shouldn't be touching it." I try to sound strong, brave, but my words come out squeaky instead.

When the angry man laughs, I reach around him to grab the precious items. His clammy hand wraps, rough as rope, *around my wrist and steals my breath. Pulling backward with all my might, I try to run away, to return to my room and wait for Mama to get out of the shower, but the angry man won't let go.*

"You've got some nerve, you little brat. Your Mama's too soft on you. I'll teach you to mind your own business." The angry man stumbles to stand, but then in a surprising fluid motion, knocks me over our footstool.

Terror rips through me, and I cry out like a cornered animal, but I can't break his hold. Only a moment more and a swish of air later, his palm connects with my bottom in a nasty swat. SMACK. Tears prick my eyes like needles, and I wriggle with all my might as he recoils his hand again and again, spanking me with enough force that my bones rattle.

CRACK. Suddenly the angry man falls backward, and Mama is there, an umbrella in her hand, her wet hair whipping like snakes around her face. The angry man collapses to the floor, rolling about, trying to right himself.

Mama leads me to the front door and shoves me out into the hall. "Go find Miss Tina. Wait for me there. Do not come back here," she demands, gripping the umbrella with both hands and slamming the door by bumping it with her hip. Then the lock clicks.

But I don't want to go. Not without Mama. I pound on the door, ear pressed to the wood, desperate to know she'll be okay. My bottom stings like I've been scorched by fire, but none of that matters.

"Nobody messes with my kid. Get out of here before I call the cops! You're a total waste of my time," Mama announces, and there is another CRASH from the apartment, accompanied by the shattering of glass. The coffee table. Loud footsteps follow, and a series of grunts. I imagine Mama fighting to hold onto her umbrella as the angry man makes use of his brute strength. Ducking to the floor, I try to see underneath the door. Nothing but shadows.

My heart stops at the next voice, deadly, deep, but also eerily calm. "Just who do you think you're talking to? Your kid ain't the only one who needs to learn a lesson."

Another loud thud, and a horrific thump against the wall. Mama's anguished cry shreds my heart to pieces. Scratching at the door, I'm in a bubble where time doesn't exist outside of

Mama's yelps. Amidst the racket, Miss Tina finds me and carries me away in her arms, though I don't go easily. I thrash and spin, desperate to help but useless. She wrestles me into her apartment and braces herself against the door to make a phone call.

Within minutes, the police arrive. Miss Tina points them to our apartment and shields me while they lead the angry man away in handcuffs. The scream of an ambulance, slowly getting louder, refuses to be ignored.

Chapter 37

1995

THE MEMORY-TURNED-NIGHTMARE stings as sharp as the angry man's swats. I bolt upright, drenched in sweat. My hair sticks to my cheeks and gets caught in my mouth. Sputtering, I rip off my covers and yank the strands from my lips. A long rattling breath later, I've managed to slow my heartbeat from a sprint to a brisk jog. The room is dark, except for a sliver of light from the hallway illuminating under my door. A rich, savory whiff of chicken slips through the crack and my stomach gurgles rebelliously in response. Dinnertime.

I run my hands through my hair like a comb, wrap my fluffy robe securely around my middle, and creak open my door. I'm gonna have to eat eventually. Why not now? But I'm hoping my family will play it cool and won't pester me for information.

Especially Aunt Julie.

Hurrying from my bedroom, I nearly careen into Lyla at the top of the stairs. She's got a wooden tray gripped tightly in her hands and an annoyed scowl plastered across her face. I can practically hear her eyes scoffing.

"Brought you some chicken noodle soup," Lyla shoves the tray in my direction. Yellow broth drips over the side of the bowl, soaking into the neighboring hunk of French bread.

Finally, a little luck! Now I won't have to eat in my family's company. But Lyla doesn't let go of her delivery. She leans over the top of the tray, so close that her hair nearly dips into the soup. Eww.

"We need to talk," she says, motioning to my room.

159

That's a first.

My mouth falls open to protest, but then I remember that I'm never speaking aloud again, not as long as I live. So, I snap it shut and shrug, wrenching the tray from her hands and carrying it to my desk. Elbows positioned comfortably on the wooden top, I dig in with abandon. Lyla closes the door behind her then sits on my bed. That should have been a clue that something was up, but I wasn't paying attention. The food was heaven on my empty stomach.

"Mom won't tell me what's going on, but you don't have to be a rocket scientist to catch the bad vibes around here," Lyla says.

Glancing over my shoulder, I see her fiddling with Grover. Before she can blink, I take the stuffed unicorn and set him atop my desk next to the tray. Lyla glares, but doesn't comment. Cue blissful silence while I munch on the French bread. Until...

"You know, Mom can be super annoying... but whatever's going on between the two of you, you shouldn't let it ruin how you feel about each other." Her voice has dropped to a whisper, and she almost sounds sincere.

Who's she kidding? Dabbing my mouth with the edge of a paper napkin, I swivel the chair until Lyla and I are face to face, my whiteboard within reach.

Are YOU honestly telling me to forgive her? Kind of hypocritical, don't you think?

I gesture toward the message like that Vanna lady from the game show with the spinning rainbow wheel.

"Hey, you can do whatever you want, but it's not good for anybody if you guys are fighting." Lyla picks at one of her fingernails while she talks, studying the pattern on my quilt.

I don't think I've ever seen her so heartfelt. This is weird.

Before I can drag the marker a single stroke across my board, Lyla's talking again. Words bubbling over, as if she popped Mentos into a mouthful of Diet Coke. The next statement drenches me, head to toe.

"I've always been jealous of you," Lyla blurts out.

I don't mean to, but I laugh. She's got to be joking. There's no one alive who would actually be jealous of me.

But she doesn't exclaim "Gotcha!" or reveal she's secretly recording me with her phone. Instead, Lyla flops back on the bed and spreads her arms like she's making a snow angel. My brain grinds to a halt, and I cap my marker. I have literally nothing to write in response, so I sit and stare. She keeps talking.

"Remember when we were little, and you used to come over for sleepovers? Mom would spend an entire day shopping, finding fun games for us to play or crafts to build. She'd drag me along, and the entire time, all she'd talk about was you. I don't think she realized how much she obsessed; it was seriously twenty-four hours straight of conversation about you."

Now Lyla laughs, but it sounds like she's choking. Like that Mentos got caught in the back of her throat on the way down. "Everything had to be perfect so that you would have fun. Mom would rant about sleepovers with her sister when they were kids, and how you are practically identical to Aunt Jenny. Sometimes, I think she forgot the two of you are different people."

Lyla sits back up and stares me straight in the eye. Neither of us blink.

"When she talked about you, I turned invisible. She didn't do it on purpose, but it was like she was using all her energy to help you. And when you came to live with us, it only got worse. You're the center of her world." Lyla's hands ball into fists, but her face stays soft and relaxed. Not mad... just honest. A Lyla I've never met.

"I know she loves me. But I also know how annoying she can be." She whisks the whiteboard from my hands and scribes:

Trust me

Her cursive stands jagged like shards of broken glass, but pretty as art. I take the board back and finally respond.

She lied to me.

Lyla wrinkles her forehead and erases the second half of the sentence with her palm, swapping her own words.

She loves you.

"And I do too. Even though sometimes you act like a bigger baby than Lucy!" She grins wide and grabs my hand. "Come with me. I've got something to show you."

Lyla pulls me into her bedroom at the end of the hall, the dim cavern, a shrine to edgy artists and emo musicians alike, every inch of her walls draped with posters of people I don't know. Lyla ushers me over to her closet and climbs atop a plastic bin nestled beneath her vast collection of black clothes. She stretches her arms high above her head and pushes a wood panel in the ceiling open. Then gripping the opening, she springs upwards from the box, disappearing into the hidden shadowy void.

This has gotten weird again.

Lyla's hand appears out of nowhere, followed by an impatient "Let's go." I mount the box and using her extra support, clamber up into the darkness.

****

The attic has clearly sat long-forgotten since dozens of cardboard boxes moved in, jam-packed into every spare inch and corner. Lyla plugs in a dusty lamp and a soft halo of yellow light makes the area less creepy, but only barely. Then she motions me over to a teetering stack of thick books that turn out to be some old photo albums. After Lyla flings a threadbare blanket across the rough wooden planks of the floor, we lie on our stomachs, and she selects the third book from the stack. Butterflies rally in my stomach but different from the ones I get with Oliver. More mysterious and tiny, like moths flitting from the shadows toward the light. My curiosity flies.

"I come up here when I want to be alone, but there are a ton of great family heirlooms to explore too," Lyla says, breathless. She flicks open the photo book cover, revealing a handwritten date on the first page. 1995. Talk about ancient. Lyla pauses as if for dramatic effect, smirking in my direction, then turns another page.

The pictures aren't black and white like I expected, but each image has a grainy quality to it like someone has covered the picture with an aging filter. The photos rest behind a protective plastic film, so it takes a second for me to figure out what I'm looking at. My mouth falls open as my brain clicks the pieces into place.

No. *Way.* There's a girl in the images, with shoulder length blond hair and a toothy crescent grin. She's posing by various exhibits at the zoo, mimicking whatever animal wanders behind her. Here's the weirdest part... the girl in the pictures is me! But that's totally bonkers, because I wasn't born until long after the millennium. My heart ba-bumps in my ears, and I point, amazed at my likeness. Lyla's still smirking. The gears grind to a stop inside my head. Have I entered an alternate dimension?

"That's Aunt Jenny," Lyla says triumphantly.

Mama? Squinting hard, I peer again at the photographs with a more discerning eye. The curve of her eyebrows and the girl's overall posture are way more relaxed than mine. No freckles either, which seals the deal. Mama could be my twin, but there are enough differences I can let out the breath I've been holding.

I shimmy the photo book across the blanket, and flip through the pages at high speed. Mama with an insanely massive five scoop ice cream cone, Mama hiking in a forest, even Mama reading a book (though the title's upside down, so I know she's posing for the picture). Each image fills a little of that empty spot inside me, stitching me together with joy and belonging.

A new girl shows up in the later pages, with dark hair and a lankier build. She's got her arm wrapped around Mama's shoulder. They're looking at each other instead of the camera, eyes crinkled like someone's just whispered an inside joke.

"And that's my Mom," Lyla says, smoothing the crinkled plastic over the image. With the two of them standing next to each other, I can see features Aunt Julie shares with Mama, similarities that make them obvious sisters. The same wide smiles and energetic posture. How could I have missed it?

"Mom loves Aunt Jenny too, and I think she misses her as much as you. That might be why she tries to take such good care of you. You remind her of her little sister." Lyla whispers, again taking my hand.

Thank you, I mouth. Lyla removes the picture of Mama and Aunt Julie from the plastic film and hands it to me. I hold it by the edges so my fingerprints don't make any smudges.

"Any time you want to come up here, feel free to storm my closet," Lyla laughs. After she's shut off the lamp, we climb down onto the plastic boxes, my heart full, but somehow much lighter than before. My loops have faded into the background as I process the strange turn of events.

As soon as I'm back in my room, I tape the picture of Mama and Aunt Julie to the inside cover of my library journal and shut the cover gently, so I don't disturb them. For the first time in a long twenty-four hours, hope blossoms in my chest.

Looks like I owe Lyla again. But this time, I don't mind.

Chapter 38

THE NEXT MORNING AUNT Julie drives Lucy and Lyla to school while I hunker in with Uncle Mars at the kitchen table. My insides are sort of hollow, maybe from all the crying, but mostly because Aunt Julie won't look me in the eyes before she leaves. I've ruminated on Lyla's comments through the night, and I can't deny that I've been really cruel to my aunt (not to mention Oliver, too). Guilt pokes me to apologize before she leaves, but fear holds me back. What if she doesn't accept my apology? What if she doesn't want anything to do with me? The anxiety weighs heavy on my heart.

Uncle Mars and I settle into our regular rhythm, him disassembling a paper-thin cell phone and me spreading my school books across the table, trying to forget how just days ago I was at least semi-successfully attending public school. I lost Mama all over again when my email came back declined, but most surprisingly, the loss of school blots out the memory. Each tick of the kitchen clock acts as a magnet tugging my attention, and reminding me what class I'd be in if I'd actually gone to school. It's hard to recall why I decided to stay home now that my loops have stopped spinning so fast.

"Hey, kiddo. Why don't we have a snack break?" Uncle Mars prompts, removing his magnifying glasses.

I stare down at my spiral before flipping it upside down. No need for Uncle Mars to investigate a blank page and wonder why my work isn't done. I click my pen methodically until I remember it's the one from Oliver and stuff it underneath my notebook so I can't see it.

Uncle Mars puts a bowl of baby carrots on the table, and I crunch on the end of one, completely lost in thought.

"Maybelline, you know that I'm here to listen if you need it, right?" Uncle Mars scoots onto the bench next to me and snags his own carrot. He puts it horizontally in his mouth, tucked between his lips, so he smiles a carrot smile.

My worry melts away, and I laugh in spite of the giant mess I've made of everything lately.

Uncle Mars tucks a hand into his jeans pocket and withdraws a yellow sticky note. He places it in my palms and wraps my fingers around it. The carrot collects in a clump at the back of my throat.

"Aunt Julie wanted me to give this to you. We've talked about how well you've done in middle school, and that it's about time we got you a cell phone, especially with your newspaper club." Uncle Mars lets go and I open my hands to see a phone number written neatly in the center of the note, next to a name: Jenny.

Mama's phone number.

"Sometimes, grown-ups think they know what's best, but like kids, we make mistakes. You used homeschool as a shield, and Aunt Julie thought keeping you separate from your Mama would protect you. You both ultimately had the same goal... even if it didn't turn out like you expected." Uncle Mars claps his hands against his lap before giving an enormous stretch. His fingertips brush against the kitchen light and make the glass tinkle like a lullaby.

I can't rip my gaze away from the post-it in my palm. Here I thought as soon as I had a number to call Mama, I'd be dialing the phone as fast as my fingers could move. I thought my major emotion would be... wholeness. Security. Hope. But my fear is still there. How can I talk to Mama on the phone if I never speak aloud again? Will she be happy to hear from me or angry that I've waited so long to call?

Do I really want her to be a part of my life?

I guess when it comes right down to it, I'm not ready to talk to her. Not yet. I stick the post-it to the inside cover of my library journal, underneath the picture of Mama and Aunt Julie. Nothing makes sense, but the fog in my brain has cleared enough that I know I'm making the right decision at this moment. Uncle Mars' voice rings through my ears.

Grown-ups make mistakes. I'd thought Mama might have been wrong before, but I never considered she was trying to do her best at the same time. Perhaps perfect doesn't exist. That flickering light I've been chasing since Mama left could be a mirage. Maybe, just maybe, I can make mistakes too and deal with the consequences.

I guess there's no easy fix, do not pass go and collect two hundred dollars, no magic answer. I'll never be able to control Mama, and I've got to be strong enough that I'm ready for anything when I dial that phone number. I don't know what will make me strong, but at the very least, I have a better understanding of how I'm feeling right now. And I'll probably make a ton more mistakes in the future, but somehow that feels okay. Imperfection doesn't have to be scary. Chomping my carrot with a satisfying crunch, I close the journal and get back to my schoolwork.

****

I've made good progress on my assignments, with the occasional sniff of the lovely library journal distracting me from looping thoughts of Oliver, middle school, Mama, and my abandoned quest to save the library. Only the opening creak of the front door breaks my concentration. Glancing at the clock, I realize that I've been hard at work for hours. Uncle Mars greets Lyla at the door, and I shut my textbook with a snap. Better late than never for lunchtime, I guess.

Lyla drops a plastic-wrapped package on the kitchen counter before grabbing a banana from the fruit bowl. Upon closer inspection, the package proves to be today's town newspaper. A tickle runs through my gut, and I remove the plastic. At the bottom of the front page I find the reminder: COUNCIL MEETING THIS THURSDAY. I rub my finger along the ink, hoping to erase the words. Lyla appears at my shoulder, reading along.

"There's still time, you know," she insists.

I toss the newspaper back on the counter and spin on my heel. There's no way I can make up with Oliver before the meeting date. I don't even know what I'd say. And I doubt he'd forgive me anyway. Better not to think about it. My feet carry me toward the stairs. It's probably time for another break on my bed, to escape reality for a bit, especially since pressure builds behind my eyes, more tears threatening to surface.

"He's still collecting signatures," Lyla adds in a rush, words flying out of her mouth and wrapping around me like a tight hug. "He worked all day at school. That bossy kid from the newspaper was helping him. And Oliver asked me how you were doing. He didn't seem mad, just sad."

Alan helping Oliver? And Oliver didn't give up on saving the library? Even after our fight, *he still cares.* That bud of hope in my chest unfurls, like a flower leaning into the sun.

Lyla approaches and jabs her finger into my shoulder. "Maybelline, you've got more power than you think. You started this mission. YOU. Are you going to finish it?"

I can only smile. Lyla rolls her eyes.

For once in my life, I don't feel alone.

Chapter 39

IT'S OFFICIAL. I'VE LOST my marbles. Two days will never be enough time to prepare a speech Oliver will have to deliver. He's not here to give any input, or encouragement, or motivation. There's absolutely no way I can do this.

Ever since Lyla mentioned that Oliver continued collecting signatures at school, a voice, like an old friend, keeps telling me that this mission is something important. And it's not Mama's voice, or Lyla's voice, or even my loops. The voice I've been hearing is my own. It murmurs in my heart, not my head. With each heartbeat thump it grows a little louder, a little more persistent, urging me into action. My heart has decided. Save the library.

The night before the council meeting, Lyla spends the entire evening in my room, pulling up videos of famous speeches on her phone so we can study and take notes. Notable speakers operate by a set of rules just like me, so at least I can find some comfort in that. Public speakers talk clearly and confidently; they keep notes in front of them but spend more time making eye contact with their audience than reading. Even though the speeches are memorized, the words don't sound rehearsed.

I've heard Oliver convince a bunch of people to sign our petition. I know in my gut that he can deliver a killer argument. He's definitely got the ingredients for success. My chest swells with pride that he's my friend, and then deflates when I remember our friendship is now a question mark because of me. I've got to show him that our time together has meant a lot to me, too. I've got to make this speech flawless.

I retrieve the pen he gifted me from my desk drawer and hold it tight in my palm. The metal glistens in the lamplight like a diamond.

Aunt Julie knocks on my door as I'm scratching lines out of my third draft. Lyla lies on the bed assembling a poster board with famous quotes she's found online:

A library is not a luxury but one of the necessities of life! - Henry Ward Beecher

Without libraries, what have we? We have no past and no future! - Ray Bradbury

(And my personal favorite.)

A library is a hospital for the mind! - Alvin Toffler

I hope it doesn't count as plagiarism to have quotes on a poster board.

Aunt Julie cracks open the door and gestures toward my nightstand. Rubbing my eyes, the blurry numbers come into focus. 11:00 PM! On a school night! I must be dreaming.

"I know you girls are hard at work, but even activists need their rest," Aunt Julie reminds us gently.

Lyla rolls her eyes before somersaulting off the bed, dragging the poster board along with her. "I'll finish it tomorrow," she says as she slides past Aunt Julie.

I stare down at my spread of potential speeches, composed of more scratch-out lines than words. Uncle Mars might let me patchwork together the final speech during homeschool tomorrow. Otherwise, I'll only have a couple of hours to iron everything out before the big meeting. I squeeze my pen so hard it might crack in half.

Aunt Julie places a hand on my shoulder, gentle as a down feather. I don't recoil from her touch, but honestly, I'm somewhere between forgiving her and still being upset. Right now, I'm too tired to decide.

"You've got this," she whispers in my ear before planting a kiss on the top of my head. A giant yawn escapes from my mouth, and I know she's right about needing rest, even though I probably would have worked through the night if she hadn't interrupted. I scoop my papers into a straight stack, change into my PJs, and surrender to sleep.

****

I'm convinced time moves faster when you secretly want it to slow down. The homeschool day is nothing more than a messy inkblot because I'm stuck rushing to finish the speech while juggling the anxiety twisting in my stomach. My loops have returned with a vengeance, spinning at full force as I try to pull the emergency brake. I practice my deep breathing, like Miss Mendoza taught me, and Uncle Mars turns on some relaxing music that actually helps me get out of my head and into the task at hand. Still, the minutes speed by, unbiased, and my hand cramps with all the writing. My normally pristine handwriting morphs into a sloppy splotch of alphabet soup. Hopefully, Oliver will be able to read the speech despite my chicken scratch.

All too soon, the rest of my family crowds in through the front door. I'm out of time. Lyla helps me collect the important papers and displays her completed poster with pride (bordering on arrogance). She's chosen bright reds and blues and yellows for the decoration and added some fiery phrases alongside the quotes. Lyla probably should have helped with the speech too, to give it the punch that it needs. Too late now.

"Alright, fam. Assemble for a pep talk." Uncle Mars gathers us in the center of the kitchen and we huddle together, arms across each other's shoulders. Lucy can't reach, so Aunt Julie kneels down to be at her level. "No matter what happens, we're in this together. You kids have shown major spunk prepping this presentation. Let's go out there and kick some council butt."

Lucy giggles and Aunt Julie frowns, but Uncle Mars winks at me, sending a burst of energy through my body. He's got my back. They all do. A warmth seeps through my limbs as I tie my shoes and gallop out the front door with my entourage in tow. I've got the library journal underneath my stack of papers... just in case.

****

I may have underestimated the size of these town meetings. Town hall takes up an entire city block, with stone spires poking holes into the sky so far above our heads that you could tweak your neck with just a quick glance. Once we enter the auditorium, a spacious dome-shaped room with marble tile, a wooden podium, and rows upon rows of seats for the audience, my heart practically stops. The council looms ahead, a group of stern elderly people situated behind a curved wooden desk. But that's not the worst part. The gathered crowd of citizens has packed shoulder to shoulder into the seats, as if the entire town conspired to attend this particular meeting. Aunt Julie gestures to a row of chairs close to the back, and we sit, the chatter of voices overwhelming me in a tidal wave.

I cover my ears, close my eyes, and focus on my breathing. In and out. In and out. We can do this. Oliver will help. Everything will be okay. A tiny squeeze on my arm brings me back to reality. Lucy's little hand grasps my forearm as she swings her feet back and forth under her chair. When she smiles, I see a shard of white poking through one of the blank spots in her gums, a new tooth coming in.

Lucy leans close and whispers, "Grover told me to wish you luck."

I take her hand and flash a real smile. The loops decelerate, if only for a moment.

Microphone feedback slices through the air, and the remainder of the audience finds their seats.

The council member in the middle, a grumpy-looking old lady, leans closer to her microphone. "Thank you for your attendance at our monthly town meeting. Salem has a strong community as its backbone, and we appreciate your participation in caring for the town. Let's run through the agenda before we start our minutes." The woman dons wire-rimmed glasses and reads from a screen on her desk. The same image pops up on a large TV mounted on the wall so the citizens can read along.

I'm distracted by a sudden urge to leap up and bolt out of the hall... to sprint past the town limits to the middle of nowhere, far away, with all this stress left in the dust. Tight bands constrict my lungs as I force myself to stay put.

Instead of listening to the drone of the councilwoman, I survey the crowd, searching for Oliver. I'm reminded of those *Where's Waldo* books from when I was a little kid. Except Oliver must be invisible, because he's nowhere to be found.

Clutching the library journal close enough to smell the comforting aroma, the meeting carries on. Occasionally, Uncle Mars and Aunt Julie shift uncomfortably in their seats, eyes flicking over to me. When your brain is in hyperdrive twenty-four seven, you notice a lot more than the average person. I don't have the words to tell them, so I pretend their concern doesn't land on my shoulders and weigh me down.

The agenda shrinks like Alice in Wonderland, and my heartbeat grows louder, so loud that I'm positive it's drowning out all other noises in the hall, even though no one's looking my way.

By the last agenda bullet point, I'm ready to scour the room on foot to find Oliver. He must be here. Lyla said he was working on the petition. There's no way he'd miss this meeting. It wouldn't make sense. But why is this knot at the back of my skull getting tighter and tighter with each passing minute? My intuition screams, *Something is wrong!*

The Q&A section is all that remains when I finally spy Oliver's dad, across the room. I allow myself a shallow breath of relief. Squinting, a terrible realization dawns on me: he's by himself. There's an empty seat next to him, but Oliver's dark curly hair is nowhere in sight. *Code red! Code red! Abort! He's not here!* The speech burns like hot coal in my hands, second only to the searing embarrassment splashed across my cheeks. Of course he wouldn't come. I've hurt him, pushed him away. He wants nothing to do with me.

Breathe in, breathe out, think, think, think. I still have the speech. I've got my cousins next to me. Lyla was literally born for this, she's a natural leader who commands attention. Surely she'll give the speech. I try to make eye contact, but she's absorbed in her phone screen, poster propped against her knees. How can she be so calm? I'll have to get her onboard on our long walk to the podium. Last-second pivot, here we come. Hopefully, I don't fall flat on my face.

What in the world have I gotten myself into?

Chapter 40

THE LEAD COUNCIL LADY calls different audience members up to the podium to ask their questions, and I fidget in my chair. A deep ache inside longs for Oliver to stand beside me at the podium. But every time I seek out his dad in the crowd, that empty chair remains empty.

All too soon, the other raised hands have dwindled, and the council lady calls for final speakers. With incredible resistance, I force my hand above the sea of heads, though I'm sure I'm trembling so hard, everyone may think I'm trying to start The Wave. She motions me forward with the tiniest glance, absorbed in whatever her colleague is whispering in her ear. I collect my papers and suck in the deepest breath of my life. This is our shot. I can't waste it.

A quick glance to my right knocks the wind out of my lungs. Now, Lyla and Uncle Mars have both vanished from their chairs. My knees knock together as I absorb Aunt Julie manning the poster, waiting patiently to accompany me to the front of the room. This *cannot* be happening. First Oliver, and now Lyla? Who's going to give the speech? I can't ask Aunt Julie, not after what I've put her through.

A ripple of panic courses through me. I would run, too, except every eye in the cavernous space has trained on me. I'm frozen stiff in terror.

Lucy hops to her feet and clasps my hand tightly, pulling me up and guiding me down the long aisle. Somehow I manage to walk, one foot feebly in front of the other. Aunt Julie follows us, smiling and waving at townspeople she knows.

The whole procession feels like an out-of-body experience, where I'm watching myself from above the crowd, completely disconnected. Lucy can't read. That leaves... me. *I* have to give the speech.

I have to talk out loud.

In front of the entire town.

There's always a moment in books where the hero has to decide whether they've got what it takes to beat the big bad monster. For a long time, I've been completely empty inside... hollow as a dead tree. I didn't have courage, or strength, or even the motivation to try to fix what was broken. And really, what's changed?

Upon reaching the second row of chairs, I pass by a familiar face: Mrs. Campbell, who gives me a sparkly wink and a nod. She pats her heart with an open palm, and I remember what she told me and Oliver in the library. *You're both bound for a big future.* Perhaps she can see some truth I can't... because she's not caught up in loops all the time. Lucy and Aunt Julie keep pace with me, and I'm reminded that I'm not alone. Strength happens together.

We've reached the podium and I've made my decision, Mama's critical voice strangely silent. One of the staff was nice enough to provide a stool for me to reach the microphone. I mount the step, shuffle my papers, but then set them to the side. This would be strike three for me and my talking rule. Am I compromising ever seeing Mama again by going through with this? Possibly. But if I don't speak, the library will definitely close. No argument. End of story. I guess this comes down to no risk, no reward. Someone coughs in the audience. Aunt Julie reaches for my speech, but I grip it tight.

Lucy's still got hold of my other hand. She pulls my floating form back to Earth, and I begin. "H—hi." More of a squeak than a word.

Aunt Julie does a double take, then spreads the poster board so the council people can see it.

The main council lady straightens in her chair and prompts, "Speak a little louder, dear."

Cold sweat breaks out at the back of my neck, but I channel my inner Mama, fanning that stubborn spark long neglected. I cross my fingers behind my back and hope Mama will be proud of me for talking, instead of disappointed.

"My name's Maybelline Reed. Salem wasn't always my home, but it is now. I love living here." Gotta make eye contact even though I'm improvising, and try to talk normal. What does that even mean? Kind of hard to know when I haven't spoken in years. But I keep going, riding my loops like a surfboard on the waves of the sea, propelling me forward. My volume grows with each uttered syllable, my muscles relaxing with each statement made.

I'm doing it.

"You mentioned earlier that this town has something special about it, and I think you're right. You called Salem a community, and I didn't know what that meant before... not really. But now I understand." I click the pen from Oliver underneath the podium as quietly as I can while I talk. Each squeeze adds a new trickle of bravery.

"For a long time, I didn't want to let anybody know me. I didn't trust anyone, and the only place I felt safe was the library. Books got me out of my head and are my friends. So when I saw in the newspaper that our library was going to close, I knew I had to fight to save it. Just like it saved me." *Big breath, Maybelline,* I remind myself as the room starts to spin. The air tastes fresh and cool as chilled water on a hot summer day.

"In trying to save the library, I've learned about community. I started middle school and met a bunch of people who wanted to help me. The newspaper club at school, ordinary citizens around town, and my... best friend, Oliver. Community means having each others' backs. And boy, they've had mine."

The audience chuckles a little. I keep going, and the words keep flowing as if a dam has broken.

"I saw community in action at the library. Oliver's dad helped fix up the building. Mrs. Campbell helped me believe in myself. And the library helps Salem learn, as our poster board shows. To abandon a part of our community goes against everything we stand for.

"Oliver and I worked on a petition to save the library, and we've got a bunch of signatures to show how much it means to the people of Salem. I hope you'll consider our request to keep it open."

A heavy slamming door makes everyone jump, and I spin around. Oliver and Lyla sprint down the long aisle, and relief rushes through me. He's here. He made it! And judging by the stack of papers in his hand, our petition has grown even bigger than I expected. The fire inside me burns brighter, lighting the way. I turn back around and face the council, making direct eye contact with each and every one of them.

"If you'd have asked me a month ago whether I would be here today, giving a speech in front of all these people, I would have run the opposite direction. But it turns out I have a voice, and I can't think of any better way to use it than saving the library." I grin at Mrs. Campbell, and she gives me a thumbs up.

"Thank you for your time." Stepping down from the stool, I give the council a bow and wrap Oliver in the biggest hug of my life.

The audience erupts into thunderous applause.

I could be the hero after all.

Chapter 41

OLIVER AND I APPROACH the stately desk as a team, handing over the petition to the council lady while the town's cheers ring through my ears.

Oliver whispers, "We have over a thousand signatures," before escorting me to my seat at the back of the room.

My loops run on, but much like Miss Mendoza's white noise machine, they blend into the background so well that I'm able to let them do their thing and keep my attention elsewhere. Mainly on the council's next move.

Finally, the council lady speaks. "Given the circumstances, the council requests a moment to review your proposition. You've made a compelling argument, and we'll consider the documents you've provided to us. This concludes our formal meeting, but feel free to stay for the final decision. Thank you, again, for your care and concern for Salem. We've heard you."

I could swear the council lady looks right at me as she's talking. The council exits through a door behind the giant desk, and chatter rolls through the ranks of audience members. No one gets up to leave. My heart has never felt more full.

My family envelops me in a group hug as we wait. Lyla doesn't even roll her eyes. When we draw away from one another, Mrs. Campbell stands patiently off to the side, a little smile playing about her lips. She's got a crinkled handkerchief clasped in her palm, but her face is dry. I float over to her as if in a dream.

"Little missy, I don't know how I'll ever be able to thank

you enough." Mrs. Campbell pats my cheek. "You truly are an inspiration."

"I meant every word," I say.

"I don't doubt it. You've got a beautiful speaking voice, dear. I hope I get to hear it more often." She disappears into the crowd, and Lyla and Oliver approach me at the same time.

"What happened to you both? I thought I lost you for a minute." My voice quivers, more from disuse than anxiety.

Oliver gives me a sympathetic glance, eyes round as saucers. I think he's still surprised to hear me talking.

"I wasn't going to make it. I sent my dad ahead, thinking I could get over here in time with the paperwork. But our printer stopped working, and I got way behind."

Oliver twirls his hoodie string around his finger. I snag it and tie both strings into a bow. He laughs.

"He texted me that he needed help, so we drove over to get him," Lyla continues.

"How did you know I'd actually speak?" I ask.

"A smart guess," Lyla smirks. "You just needed a push in the right direction."

"Thanks," I mumble, but I mean it. Lyla seriously surprised me. She melts into the crowd the next moment, heading toward one of her friends. Leaving me and Oliver... alone.

"I'm sorry," I begin.

"I'm sorry," Oliver says at the same time.

I scratch the back of my head, both of us giving an awkward laugh. "You didn't do anything wrong. I went a bit bonkers." My voice sounds weird to my ears, but it feels so good to let my apology free.

"Happens to the best of us," Oliver replies. "When I heard you were brave enough to stand up in front of all these people, it helped me be brave enough to face my own fear." His gaze tilts downward, shoulders slouched. "Until I met you, I hadn't been able to ride in a car since Mom's car accident. That first time driving to the playground, I was super scared. But this time, your bravery was contagious."

"So, we both needed the library... and we need each other," I whisper. The butterflies in my stomach must have doubled in size because their jumbo wings tickle me all over. I suppress a laugh.

Oliver leans a little closer. "Maybelline, I..."

And just at that moment, the council returns. I'm a mix of excitement to hear their decision and disappointment that Oliver didn't finish his sentence. Something about the way he said my name held the weight of the world hidden inside. We take our seats, and Lucy sits atop Uncle Mars' lap so we have enough chairs since it's still standing room only. Not a single person has left, as far as I can see.

Oliver locks elbows with me as the council lady approaches the microphone.

"Thank you for your patience. We've reviewed the submitted petition, and while impressive, we've decided to move forward with our relocation of the library, as the new plot has been purchased and we're ready to break ground."

A collective gasp shudders across the audience, and my heart falls into my stomach. We failed. My library will still close. I choke back a sob. Oliver pats my back, eyes trained ahead, unblinking.

"However, in light of recent events and the additional filed paperwork, the original library building must be preserved in its current state. We accept the filing for historic registry on the new evidence presented."

Additional filed paperwork? New evidence? I stir and shift closer to the edge of my seat, holding my breath, while Oliver grins a mysterious grin.

"Seeing that the original library once belonged to a notable journalist, Mr. Edward Baker, of the New York Post..."

"That's my great-great-great grandfather!" a nearby voice shouts. Alan from the school newspaper stands triumphantly on the seat of his chair, waving to the council with both hands.

A man beside him shakes his head and tugs Alan back down.

"Thus, the old library qualifies for historic registry status. The building will be preserved and protected for generations to come. We'll be starting a committee of like-minded citizens to head the library project, where we will repurpose the old building into something new, for the community to enjoy. I invite any interested individuals to join us next week to brainstorm ideas." Again, the council lady stares straight at me as she speaks.

All I can do is blink. For once my loops have ground to a halt. What is going on? Some sort of miracle is at work here, and its name is Oliver.

"Thanks again for your attendance. You make Salem the best it can be." The council lady turns off her mic and leads the council group out of the auditorium.

I'm still trying to catch up, gaping like a fish out of water.

"Surprise!" Oliver exclaims.

"What just happened?" I ask, pinching my thigh to be sure I'm awake.

"When I was collecting signatures at school, Alan mentioned that the library used to be a house that belonged to one of his famous ancestors, some big shot journalist who moved to New York. My dad brought up the historic registry before, so I talked to him about how to file for the library to be considered. Alan helped, almost too much, with getting the details about his famous great-great-great grandfather right. The application is still pending, but I put it at the bottom of the petition anyways." Oliver shrugs like he hasn't just moved a mountain.

I bite my tongue to keep from crying and pull him into another tight hug. "You did it! I can't believe it."

"I never would have made it in time if you hadn't delivered the speech. We did it." Oliver gives me a double high-five, and that flicker of hope in my chest erupts into a full-blown explosion.

Two ordinary sixth-grade kids managed to save the library. I couldn't have written a better ending if I tried.

Mama would be proud. I know it.

Chapter 42

"HOW ABOUT PIZZA TO celebrate?" Aunt Julie motions our entourage into a clump at the back of the hall while the rest of the patrons filter out the double doors.

Lyla appears, "Let's invite Mrs. Campbell too."

Aunt Julie catches her on our way to the car and my heart fills to bursting.

I watch as Oliver squares his shoulders to enter the passenger side of his dad's truck. If he was looking, I'd give him an encouraging thumbs up. The truck engine grumbles to life, and they turn down Main Street toward Mario's. If pride translated into energy, I'd be glowing like a neon firefly. I can't believe how much Oliver has changed since I met him. Though, I guess I've changed too.

"Meghan told me some people like stinky fish on their pizza! Blech!" Lucy exclaims, bouncing in her carseat.

"I once had a pizza with marshmallows and gummy bears!" Uncle Mars chimes in.

I swear Lucy starts drooling, her eyes full of wonder.

"You can't believe everything you hear, Luce," Lyla responds. For once, Lyla's phone rests tucked in her pocket.

"Everyone knows deep dish is the best kind of pizza," I add.

The car goes utterly quiet, except for the change jingling in the glove box.

I retract back into my shell a bit. It could be that my family isn't ready for me to talk all the time. I don't want to make them uncomfortable.

Aunt Julie recovers fastest. "You're a girl after my own heart." She punctures the tension with the radio on-button and we sing along to a familiar song about country roads. Music to my ears!

****

As expected, Mario doesn't disappoint. The table practically bows in the middle when he brings out the food—deep dish cheese, thin crust sausage, meatballs, fried ravioli, mozzarella sticks, and even a few complimentary family-style pastas.

Oliver sits to my left and Lyla to my right, but we've got the corner of the restaurant to ourselves, so it's easy to see everybody. Mostly I stuff my face with Italian food and try to keep up with the back-and-forth chatter. My loops have gone silent in the midst of this warm togetherness. I'm not sure what that means, but at this moment, I feel like I've conquered the world. With my community. With my family who loved me all along.

The realization sings in my chest, flowing outward and blooming into a symphony of gratitude.

My loops held me hostage for such a long time. Not anymore. I may not be able to control the world, but I can control who I let in mine.

****

"Will you be at school tomorrow?" Oliver asks when we say goodnight in the parking lot.

"Wouldn't miss it," I whisper. "I've got some catching up to do."

Oliver grins. "Just be ready. Alan will tell you his great-great-great grandfather's entire life story."

"Considering we owe his great-great-great grandfather, I'll allow it this time."

Oliver swoops in for another hug (again, I'm not complaining), his cheeks illuminated red in the glow of the street lamps, though that could be my imagination. We part ways, but before I can get in the car, Aunt Julie taps me on the shoulder.

"What do you say to a walk?" she asks.

For a night in autumn, there's no chill. The crickets chirp

and the frogs croak peacefully, and I can't find any of that old anger inside, so I nod, and we head down the sidewalk toward home. My cousins make faces at us through the car window as Uncle Mars drives by.

"Your Mama and I used to go on nighttime walks when we were kids. We'd sneak out of the house through our bedroom window and creep around the block, pretending we were the only people on Earth."

Aunt Julie grabs a drifting maple leaf from the air, twirling it between her fingers. She gestures to a bench set off the path, and I follow obediently, listening. Over the sparse treetops, I can see the angled roof of the library in the distance. There's great comfort in knowing the roof won't be going anywhere.

"Maybelline, I didn't know how to help your Mama." Aunt Julie hands me the maple leaf when she turns to face me. "It was like she and I spoke different languages, and the older we grew, the bigger the distance became between us. Losing her was like losing my best friend." Aunt Julie swipes underneath her eye, but I don't interrupt.

"I thought when you came into our lives that it was my chance to make amends... to answer for my inability to help your Mama out of her bad habits. But I can see now that as I was trying to protect you, I also isolated you. My choices weren't fair. I hope you can forgive me."

"You've given me everything, Aunt Julie," I say, matter-of-fact, blowing the maple leaf from my hand into the air, where it flutters as if tugged by invisible strings. "You gave me a home. I think when I was little, I was trying to fix Mama, too. But it's impossible to fix other people, 'cause they have to want to fix themselves, you know? All we can do is love them."

Aunt Julie runs her palm along my hair, and I lean back to count the stars. I make it to thirty-three before she speaks again.

"When you were born, there were complications," she says. "The doctors told your Mama she was in danger if she kept laboring, that they would need to operate, which would put you in jeopardy. Your Mama looked them dead in the eye and said, 'I know my baby, and there's no way you're putting her at risk.' She chose to keep laboring, and sure enough, you were born the next morning. The process took a toll on her, but you wouldn't know it. Looking at you, she had stars in her eyes."

My breath catches in my throat. That's not the story Mama always told me. Mama... protected me? She wanted me safe and sound? Mama loved me.

Or... Mama loves me.

Aunt Julie wraps an arm around my shoulders and gives them a squeeze. Fresh tracks of tears flow down both our faces.

"We'll get you your cell phone and you can talk regularly to your Mama. I'm thinking we may invite her to the holidays this year, too, so long as you feel ready. I'll leave the decision up to you."

"Thanks, Aunt Julie." If she wasn't holding me tight, I could probably float up into the clouds and fly all the way home.

Chapter 43

"BE SURE TO ADD 'plaque' and make it BIG. Better yet, gold, if possible." Alan leans over my shoulder while I write, his grating voice disrupting the peace of Tuesday afternoon's newspaper meeting.

To be honest, Oliver and I haven't exactly stayed on task... but I don't think Ms. Bennett minds. Word traveled fast about the town meeting, and teachers and students alike want to know how they can be involved in Project Library. The council scheduled the first brainstorming meeting for later this week, so Oliver and I are determined to get our best ideas written out to present.

Ms. Bennett asked us to write our article for the school paper on our experience at the council meeting, which was so easy I finished it in one sitting. All that's left is proofreading, which Oliver has generously agreed to do.

"I think it's required for them to put plaques on historic registry buildings," Oliver raises an eyebrow at Alan.

"You can never be too careful. I'm the chief safety officer after all," Alan spouts.

Oliver and I exchange a glance.

Alan doesn't notice. "Besides, great-great-great gramps was instrumental in putting Salem on the map. His name should be at the top of the plaque."

"How about this," I say. "We suggest that a section of the town museum be dedicated to your family history. That way, there's an entire wing of recognition."

Alan's eyes bulge out of their sockets, and he slaps me on the back. "I like how you think, Reed. If you need to bounce around any more ideas, I'll be fine-tuning my article for the paper." Alan retreats to his desk, all smiles.

Oliver and I release a simultaneous breath of relief.

"Do you think they'll bite on the town museum idea?" Oliver asks, scooting his chair closer to me. The smell of fresh grass tickles my nose and tilts up the corners of my mouth.

"Sure, why not? I think Salem deserves a museum, and it's a great way to get the rest of the community involved." I set down my clicky pen without a click and run a hand through my hair. My loops whir in the background like a spinning fan. But I'm far too busy to worry about what they're buzzing about. We've got important work to do.

"Oh, I almost forgot. Check this out." Oliver digs around in his backpack and pulls out a padded black case. He tugs open the zipper to reveal a bunch of fancy looking lenses and a shiny black camera. "My dad gave me some of my mom's camera equipment. She was a professional photographer. He thought I could practice and take pictures of Salem for the newspaper." Oliver hefts the camera from its case, wraps the strap around his neck, and messes with a few of the buttons on top. His hands become still and he stares at the camera, contemplating.

"Mom wouldn't go anywhere without this thing. We used to tease her about how she'd take so many pictures." His low voice carries grief, but also... admiration.

"I think it's awesome you could follow in her footsteps. Ms. Bennett would probably let you take pictures for the paper too. It's in your blood, after all."

He brightens at my suggestion and packs the camera carefully away.

"Are you free this weekend? We could pick some landmarks to photograph, if you want." His voice has gone squeaky. Nervous. And he's looking at me weird, like he's never seen me before. Heat rises to my cheeks, and the classroom's gone stifling. My tongue sticks to the roof of my mouth.

"I'm supposed to go shopping with Lyla for a costume for the Halloween dance," I mumble, packing up my papers and finding particular interest in the pattern on my shoelaces.

"Can I go with you?" Oliver asks.

"Shopping? I'd love that. It'll be nice to have something to do other than be Lyla's walking shopping cart." I grin.

Oliver looks me straight in the eye. "I meant... do you want to go to the dance... together?"

I'm caught like a fly in the most hypnotic sapphire webs. I open my mouth, but no words come out. *Get it together, Maybelline.* What would Mama do?

"Sure. Sounds fun," I croak.

Oliver's eyes sparkle. My loops twirl on and on about how crowded the dance will be, and how Lyla will tease me for a century if we go as a pair. But, to be honest, I don't care about any of that stuff—not nearly as much as having fun with Oliver. *Big breath, in and out.* My anxiety loosens its grip.

At the stroke of four, we shuffle down the empty hallway to the exit, and my red chariot awaits, Uncle Mars rocking out behind the wheel, waiting to take me to therapy. Oliver snaps open his skateboard and gives me a high five before rolling away. I play with a button on my shirt while I watch him go.

"Take some pictures on your way home!" I holler at him.

He answers with a thumbs up and a dazzling smile.

When I pop open the car door, Uncle Mars turns his blaring music all the way down.

"Hey! My favorite sixth grader! Ready to go, kiddo?"

I buckle my seat belt with a snap while Oliver whizzes away out of the corner of my eye. "Yeah, I think I am."

****

The lively flame flickers on Miss Mendoza's newest scented candle: Pumpkin Banana Bread. I take a big, sweet gulp of air as I sit down, making a mental note to ask Aunt Julie if we can make some for breakfast.

Miss Mendoza cracks her window open before settling in her armchair. The whoosh of the traffic and whistling breeze overpower her white noise machine but calm me just the same.

"Did you bring your notebook?" Miss Mendoza asks with a fond smile, and I brandish the leather-bound journal in front of me. "Aunt Julie filled me in about your new cell phone. I'm proud of you for paying attention to your feelings and knowing you aren't ready to talk to your Mama yet. That being said, are you open to trying something new to help?"

I nod.

"I know you haven't wanted to take medication before, but with the amazing progress you've made so far, I think it would be the cherry on top. It may be the next step toward meeting up with Mama, face to face. How would you feel about trying a small dosage? Obviously, we'll get your aunt and uncle's approval first." Miss Mendoza taps her pen once on her clipboard as she studies me.

"Oliver takes medicine because he gets so sad about his mom," I answer.

"Different medicines do different things. I'm glad that Oliver has the support he needs to feel better."

I bounce a finger on my chin and decide. Miss Mendoza hasn't steered me wrong yet. "We can try it. So long as it's not a lot."

Miss Mendoza jots a quick note on her paper and sets her clipboard to the side.

"All right, on to the main event. What have you got for me today?"

I flip open my notebook, enjoying the texture of the pages between my fingers and taking a quick whiff of its musty library scent, books and secrets and peace, all jumbled into one.

"Let's start with your original list and then read through your new one," she says.

I read aloud, which turns out is pretty fun to do. I'm good at it, too.

Things I'd like to change:

 Going to middle school

 Mama

 ★*Lucy's drawing*

Things I'd like to stay the same:
The library

Gazing at the old list is like looking backward through time. I remember writing these words, but I'm shocked because they no longer fit me, similar to a pair of jeans that's gotten way too short. Thinking about the old me may be uncomfortable but makes me proud too. I've grown, and I'm still growing. It makes me curious to see how much I'll have grown by next year.

"Do you mind reading your new list?" Miss Mendoza rests her elbows on her knees, hands under her chin, as birdsong drifts in through the window.

Things I'd like to change:
My anxiety
My self-doubt
My repetitive loops
The paint color in my room

Things I'd like to stay the same:
Middle School
My family
My friendship with Oliver
Living in Salem
Mama

Miss Mendoza nods along like I'm singing the best song she's ever heard. I trace over my cursive with my fingertip. It's not quite perfect… but it's mine. Neat and a little wiggly at the edges. Hope lives in the wiggles that I used to erase. The birdsong gets louder. A quick peek out the window reveals a full-grown robin staring in, white feathered star upon its chest. The chick I put back in the nest, my robin. It gives me a chirp before launching into the cobalt blue sky—free.

I bet the next time I write this list, even more will have changed. I used to think change was the worst part of being alive, but I've learned sometimes change can mean better things are coming.

Part of me wishes I could talk to six-year-old me and tell her everything is going to be okay. I don't know if she would have believed me with her loops twisting like a tornado. But the proof lies inside today-me, in the gaps within the loops. And the more holes I've embraced, the less important my worries have become.

Perhaps those holes of imperfection don't need filling—they let the people who matter inside.

Never underestimate the power of a good loophole.

Maybelline's Coping Skills Toolbox

- Deep breathing
- Meditation (guided imagery): "Picture filling a balloon with each breath."
- Mindfulness: remember I'm strong even when I get worried
- Self-affirmations: "I'm proud of me." "I'm really smart." "I'm a good friend."
- Journaling: write lots of stories about my feelings
- Get sassy with my loops (talk back)
- Put worries "on hold" until later
- Five senses grounding exercise (scavenger hunt): find something I can hear, something I can see, something I can touch, something I can taste, and something I can smell
- Counting grounding exercise: count my breaths, or Lucy's giggles, or Lyla's eye rolls
- Get active: skateboard with Oliver, go for a jog, try a sport, dance around, jump rope, or climb a tree
- Fun activities: listen to music, read lots of books, tinker with Uncle Mars, draw with Lucy, watch a funny movie, and bake with Aunt Julie
- Make a calm down kit: relaxing music playlist with ear buds, stress ball, lots of clicky pens, my library journal, pictures of happy memories, fidget toys

Acknowledgments

This book is dedicated to anyone who has ever gone unheard.

Books evoke a sense of community and remind us that we're not alone. No matter the distance between us or difference in our walks of life, stories connect us emotionally through a shared reading experience. I'm so grateful to my tight-knit community for helping me bring Maybelline's story to life.

Thank you, first and foremost, to my downright amazing parents for raising me with unconditional love. Thank you to my sister and best friend, Sarah Ann Doughty, for the inside jokes, constant companionship, tough love, and, oh yeah, incredible art! I mean, have you seen my gorgeous cover and chapter art? You never cease to amaze me. Thank you to my superhero husband, Dan, for loving me and showing me how to love myself. Thank you to my ray-of-sunshine daughter, Ana, for inspiring me everyday, and teaching me to be a better human being. Thank you to my in-laws and extended family for believing in me and supporting my writing dreams at all the twists and turns. I owe each and every one of you a debt of gratitude. And to Dennis Doughty, I'll miss you dearly and I'm so grateful to call you family. I know you've still got my back.

Many thanks to my online community of writer friends and colleagues who help me hone my craft: the incomparable #MGpies who pick me up when I feel hopeless, fellow author Sarah McKnight for being the best critique partner a girl could ask for, the entire #WritingCommunity on Twitter/X for always chasing their dreams, and my fantastic publisher, Artemesia Publishing (imprint: Kinkajou Press), for recognizing how special Maybelline is and giving her voice a platform.

A huge shout-out to the readers who shaped this book into the finished product: Kristi Wright, Aisling Fowler, Christiana Doucette, Brenda Miller, Neal Romriell, Anna Ejoh, Miriam Spitzer Franklin, Heather Morris, Denise Dra-

Weber

peau, "Gogos Buzz" Cilla, Mike Shiffer, Ruth Mallon, Kate Derbishire, Martha Plunk Ward, and Aspen K. Somers. Major thanks to Catherine Arguelles, Stephanie Lupo Henson, and Meg Eden Kuyatt for reading my ARC and providing blurbs. And to any reader I've forgotten, I'm more thankful than I can say.

Thank you to the caring, dedicated therapists I've visited over the years, especially Cindy Miller, who helped me find and accept myself, broken pieces included. Thanks to anyone in the mental health or education fields who advocate for quiet and invisible children. Keep persevering. These kiddos need you.

Finally, much gratitude to the past, present, and future readers who shadow Maybelline as she finds her voice. I don't know you personally, but I believe in you. If you need a listening ear, you can reach me at rebeccaweberwrites@gmail.com. You are not alone.

And never forget, your voice matters.

Author's Note

Dear Readers,

I'm showing my age here, but let's rewind to when I entered first grade, good ol' 1995, after my family moved to a completely new community and I enrolled in a completely new school. I was a shy kid to begin with, but the move was extra hard on me socially.

I remember an incident in first grade where I poked a kid with a stick to get them to move and had to apologize publicly, much to my incredible shame. I also recall my first grade teacher telling us not to raise our hands in the middle of a lesson, which inevitably led to my only potty accident ever at school, an event you'll no doubt recognize from Maybelline's flashbacks.

As elementary school progressed, I clammed up even more. I remember answering a question aloud in fourth grade, to which one of my classmates responded, "I didn't know you could talk!" Long story short, much of Maybelline's social anxiety comes from my own personal experiences.

Sometimes mental/emotional health problems don't make sense. I grew up with a fantastic family unit. My parents loved me and encouraged me no matter what, but I always had anxiety bubbling underneath the surface. When I entered middle school, I cried during my school tour because I was so overwhelmed. My family and I didn't really know any better; I was just the kid who worried too much.

When I finally tried therapy, well into my college years, lo-and-behold, I was diagnosed with OCD and anxiety. There was a name for my constant worry and looping trains of thought. My nervous normal was something I could actually improve. But it would take a lot of work and courage.

As an adult, I've committed myself to facing my anxiety

head-on and being completely transparent about my journey. Many of the calming tools you read about in Maybelline's story are actual coping strategies for anxiety. It only took me 20+ years to figure them out! I'm overjoyed that therapy is now a mainstream option for anyone struggling to figure themselves out. The world has come a long way in recognizing that invisible struggles are just as real as physical ailments. For that, I'm grateful.

If you take nothing else from *Loophole*, I hope you realize you aren't alone in your struggles. Therapy is a great option for viewing yourself from an unbiased perspective and finding coping strategies that work specifically for you. Plus, it's darn helpful having someone to talk with about your feelings. Your voice matters, even if you might feel otherwise. You're stronger than you think.

Sincerely,
An anxious (and proud of it) author

If you or anyone you know experiences domestic abuse, please call The National Domestic Violence Hotline (800) 799-7233, or text BEGIN to 88788.

Author Bio

Rebecca is a Midwestern girl with a lifelong passion for books! She spends most of her time nurturing her baby girl and two Boston Terrier fur-babies, and flipping houses with her realtor husband. It took fifteen years to find the courage to craft her first novel, *The Painter's Butterfly*, but now she's never letting her feather pen go! While she misses teaching preschool-aged children their ABC's, Rebecca is thrilled to have the chance to reach middle graders worldwide with her fantastical stories. *Loophole* is her second published novel.